PEACE

layla Audeamus

Peace
Copyright © 2023 by layla Audeamus

All rights reserved. No part of this book may be reproduced
or transmitted in any form or by any means, electronic or
mechanical, including photocopying, recording, or by any
information storage and retrieval system without express
written permission from the author, except in the case of
brief quotations embodied in critical reviews and certain
other noncommercial uses permitted by copyright law.

Printed in the United States of America.

Brilliant Books Literary
137 Forest Park Lane Thomasville
North Carolina 27360 USA

Table of Contents

Acknowledgements

For a dear, sweet friend who helped to steer me in the right direction;

The loves who are no longer here but the one who came and rescued me from a formless, Masterless existence, I've given you my body, behavior, and attitude and you accepted.

Forward

Some things you will read about in this, the last book of the trilogy, will seem strange to you. When the idea of consensual slavery is mentioned, you need to get past the traditional ideas of coerced slavery in times past. It means exactly what it says, consensual slavery. The consensual part means the person giving themselves is doing it willingly without coercion from anyone. In a Master/slave relationship, the slave is there because they want to be and need to be.

The M/s lifestyle as depicted in this book is much like the one, I lived in with my late Master/husband. For almost eight years I not only willingly but happily gave him total control over me in every facet of my life. I gave him my body, behavior, and attitude. He gave me love, cared for me, took care of me, and protected me. I trusted him to keep me safe both physically and emotionally. I gave him control over me because I did not want it.

Now, do not think that slaves like myself are *doormats* for a Master to walk all over, use, abuse, and cast aside. Far from it. Under him I pursued not just one but two Master's degrees and a PhD, plus wrote more than eight books. He was my primary supporter to study and write as much as I wanted. I could have done anything and he would have been cheering me onward. We both agreed, however, that our relationship was more important and it always came first. Having said that, he was the one backing me up on the nights and weekends when a paper was due, a book needed another chapter, or I needed to vent about a particularly difficult assignment.

You may also notice some naming conventions which are different. As practiced by the people we were friends with in the lifestyle, a collared sub or slave's first name is always in lower case letters. Alice is the main character and her name is capitalized until she is collared by David when her name is simply written as alice. The ceremony may also give you pause but don't let it. What happens in a collaring ceremony is all consensual. Each group has their own protocol and each Master has his own wishes. Branding, both hot and cold, tattooing, affixing of labia rings or tags, and any of a myriad of things can be done. For some Master's the collar is the only thing they want but for others they want more. It is all consensual and the slave wants it just as much if not more than her Master. She is proud of his ownership of her.

Before the Peace

The text message from Alice on David's phone was simple

"I can't do this because I don't love you. Goodbye."

David's Agony

Amara tried to calm his friend. "Look, this may be, uhm, pre-wedding jitters. Let's go to the hotel and I'll see what Evie might know. She's with Alice so maybe we can get some answers."

They dressed and David let Amara drive. "Look my friend you are in no shape to drive," Amara said as he slid behind the wheel. They passed the time in silence except when David had to give directions for Amara to get to the hotel where the girls were supposed to be staying.

David was devastated. Alice was his, he had trained her, she had given him her virginity, and pledged to first, be his submissive and later, had asked to be his consensual slave. They had the new house and much of the furniture were things she had saved from her family home. They were making a life together. What had happened?!

Amara didn't know about David's other, lifestyle life, he only knew him as a top cardiologist and good friend. David couldn't tell him about his dark side, nobody, not even Alice had seen all of it but she loved him in spite of his dark desires. Now, where, how, what had made her call it all off? He'd been trying her phone. He needed, had, to talk to her. At first it went to voice mail and then, it said the box was full and hung-up. He threw his phone on the floor but then picked it up to call his father, David wanted him to contact his cousin George who was a detective in the police. He needed to find Alice.

When the two arrived at the hotel, Evie was just waking up. She didn't know anything about what was going on and the way David was behaving, he was close to deep despair. Amara sat him down while Evie had a chance to dress. By the time she came back into the room from her bedroom, David had become cold and steely. It was his doctor persona, the one that did what had to be done and either gave good or bad news to a waiting family.

Evie had the extra key-card to Alice's suite and she led the men there. The place was a mess. Her wedding dress was on the floor and she could see some dirty shoe prints on it. Her purse was still in the closet where she had put it the night before when they had come from the dinner. Her phone was not on the charger but another bag which had been on the table was missing too.

David sniffed the air. It didn't smell like Alice but a different but familiar smell was layered on top of hers'. Chloroform, sweet smelling but very distinctive. It had been used in years past by surgeons but medicine and anesthesiologists had moved on from it to better things. Now, only people who didn't care what they did to someone used it. He looked around the room again, in the bedroom the dress was on the floor, and he was sure that Alice had not left this room of her own free will. Someone had taken his beloved and now they would pay!

"Don't, uh don't touch anything. I think someone has taken her or hurt her." Looking at Amara, "do you smell it, the chloroform?" Talking to no one in particular, "whoever has her is dead, she didn't leave me, she was stolen!"

A sharp rap on the door and Amara opened to find Mr. Khoury, David's father, and another, younger man with him. David recognized his cousin George. "I'm glad you came, we didn't touch anything, but I think she's not just missing, she didn't run away, she's been taken. Smell the chloroform? You have to find her!"

George pulled out his phone and punched in some numbers. "Hello, this is George Khoury, I'm a detective with Green Valley PD. I need to talk to your chief of detectives." He listened then replied, "I know it's Saturday, but I'm standing in a hotel room and the girl who was supposed to be marrying my cousin this evening is missing and it looks and smells like she has been taken." He waited again, "Yep, possibly kidnapped. And I need some forensic people over her right away to look at this room before it can be contaminated by a bunch of plods running in and out."

David's father had taken him aside and given his boy a hug. Alex Khoury had never been a demonstrative man, but the grief he knew his son was experiencing was enough to melt anyone's heart. "Look son, let the police take this. We need to let them do their work, okay?" David nodded and Alex Khoury told George they would be down the hall in Evie's suite. Amara took Evie and Alex took his son to a place where they could wait.

Alex ordered coffee and breakfast from room service then went into the bedroom to call his wife. It didn't look as if there would be a wedding that day and things needed to be done to stop the people from going into an empty museum expecting to attend David's nuptials. The member of the family who kept the family database had only needed to be told about the situation when a mass email message was sent to the members of the Khoury family who'd been invited. David looked at his phone and did the same to his group of Doms and Masters who had been invited and especially for those who would be expecting to witness his collaring ceremony the next evening.

Coffee and breakfast arrived when Evie's laptop beeped. She hadn't looked at her machine since this whole thing had happened and she was on edge. She opened her laptop and saw the strange return address but a message that purported to be from Alice. The message simply read, "Ask David why he would sell me?".

Evie screamed as she backed away from the table. Her eyes went from the screen to David and back again. Shaking, she pointed at David, "you, you, you" she was breathing raggedly and her eyes were wide and she was frantic. "You, what have you done to her? Where is she?" Amara put his arms around her to calm her but now she was sobbing and yelling at the same time.

Alex looked at the screen and David peered over his shoulder. When his father had read the message he twisted around to peer at his son, he found the man looking back at him but wasn't sure if he really had ever seen him. "What does this mean, son, It's crazy but what did you do to that poor girl?"

David was trying to digest what was on the screen himself. He knew though, he knew who had Alice and what he would have to do to save her. He took his cell phone and went into the bedroom and closed the door leaving a sobbing Evie, a distraught Amara, and his father to simply watch him leave.

Once inside, he called a member of the group Master Avery had belonged to in Boston. Master Mark had spoken at Avery's funeral a few months back and David had remembered him from when he had been a young man of promise whom his uncle had recommended to the Doms and Masters of this particular group of gentlemen. After telling him who he was, David asked Mark about Damian and the club he owned, Arabesque.

Mark cleared his throat and paused. "Master Mark, I know Damian from med school and he has this crazy idea that I owe him a life because he was sent down for cheating in a class when we were roommates. The professor is the one who caught him, not me, but he has blamed me for all of it all these years. At Master Avery's wake he told me he was going to make me pay." David paused before going on, "uh, this evening I'm supposed to get married." Emotion was creeping into his voice, "but, uh, my girl, the girl I was going to marry has been taken and I think Damian has her."

David tried to control his voice but with great difficulty, "a few minutes ago, an email with the word "Arabesque" in the address from where it was sent, just says, "Ask David why he has sold me." That sounds like Damian to me." David was shaking and fought to regain some control. "Please Master Mark, where is Arabesque and how can I find Damian."

Suddenly, the call to Master Mark was cut and another voice broke in. "David, David Khoury?" a clipped, professional sounding man asked. "My name is Cecil White and I'm with Houndsford Security. We have a client, a Miss Alice Blake who has you listed as an emergency contact. Can you identify yourself please?"

David shook his head, he was on the phone trying to find his girl and now this guy breaks in, how does that happen? "Look mister, uh, whoever, I was on the phone with someone trying to find my fiancé. If you need to identify me, I'm the man whose bride was stolen from her hotel room by an evil man. I'm trying to find her and how the fuck did you get on my line anyway?"

"Okay, I think you have identified yourself sufficiently, but I still have to ask. Give me your license number." David was beside himself but complied. "Excellent, first we know where she is but not how she got there. She has a GPS tracker on her and it went active in the last thirty minutes." David began to think clearer, this guy is telling him he knows where she is.

"I need to go and get her before something bad, and I mean even worse than being kidnapped, can happen. I think I know who took her and why but the why is not the issue right now, the getting her back ASAP is the only thing and right the fuck NOW!" David didn't usually use such language but it was Alice and sometime nicely, nice filters be damned!

"Okay, we got you. Now, I've contacted our office in Boston and they will have eyes on this place where she is being held, or is, whatever. I'm headed up that way and if you want to come along, go to general aviation and you'll see a black jet with a dog's head on its tail. That's me, my crew, and one really irate lawyer. Please be here soon because we're leaving."

Detective George Khoury knocked on the suite door. Amara answered and told him where to find David. Entering the bedroom, he found his cousin on the phone but finishing up the call. "You were right, we have footage of her being taken by a couple of guys, looks like private security types with a man and woman. They went out the back but the cameras got them." He pulled out his phone and brought up the stills taken from the film.

Alice looked passed out but knowing about the chloroform he knew she wasn't drunk. A pair of big, burly guys were holding her up, feet barely touching the ground. The second picture made David flinch. God he was even looking at the camera, Damian and beside him, Rachel. It was the look on Damian's face that chilled him and fired his anger. He was wanting David to know who had his love and was taunting him to come and get her.

"Come on, you got a car with a siren?" George nodded. "Good, I need to get to the airport, fast, and I'll fill you in on the way." David was all but pushing his way out of the room. Alex stood looking at the determination on his son's face as he pulled him aside. "Dad, we know where she is and I'm going with some security guys to get her. Stay here, try to shut all of this down until I get my girl. I love you and tell mom."

Alex nodded at his son and got back on his phone. A uniformed policeman was outside of the door to Evie's suite and another plainclothes man was entering to take statements. David cared for none of that, only to get his little Alice home where she belonged.

David had never ridden in a police car, especially not one with a siren blaring. He filled in cousin George on the way to the airport and as his cousin stopped at general aviation. They saw before them a large black jet, gold lettering down the side, "Houndsford Security International", and a stylized dog's head on the tail. A steward was standing at the bottom of the stairs seemingly waiting for David. His cousin took a small bag from his trunk and pressed it into David's hands. "You need a shave cuz, this should do you okay." They shook hands and David went up the stairs. George stood by his car door and watched as the stairs were folded up into the jet, the door closed, and the jet-engines spun up. Within minutes the plane was on a runway and shooting into the clear, cloudless sky.

Alice: for Sale

Alice lay on the sofa for several minutes, alone in the office of this man named Damian. She was almost afraid to move. She looked at the wall near the sofa and realized a recessed door was hidden there. Quietly and gingerly, she got up to try it. There was no handle but by pushing it, it opened enough for her to get her hand in.

A light came on and beyond the door she saw a massive and manly bathroom. It had the biggest shower she had ever seen, a free-standing tub fit for two large people, and a bank of three separate sinks on a white enamel vanity. The whole room was white and almost clinical. The toilet was in a separate room off of the main bath with a toilet and bidet.

Alice needed the toilet but the labia clips were too tight. She removed them and breathed a sigh. This whole thing was nuts. David didn't, couldn't have sold her, not to this guy or to anyone. She was his, he was hers, nothing made sense. She finished and washed her hands. In the mirror above the sink, she saw a fluffy white bathrobe hanging on the back of the door. She put it on and closed the door.

She heard the door click as a key was put in the door. Angry voices could be heard beyond. "I'm not giving her to you and that's it!" It was Damian and the anguished scream must have been the woman, Rachel.

The door opened and the two looked at Alice in the bathrobe. Rachel was the first to move, "you little whore, where are the clips we put on you, who do you think you are taking things that don't belong to you?" The woman was in a rage and she raised her arm, the one with the riding crop in her hand, and was about to strike Alice.

Alice turned to dodge the blow and Damian shouted at Rachel. "Enough, enough!" Damian stepped forward and took the crop from Rachel's hand. Alice saw him make the hand-gesture to kneel and Rachel sank to her knees before Damian. "You will not do anything to my property, do you understand?"

Rachel, eyes lowered, "yes, Master Damian."

"Good, I don't want this parcel hurt or damaged. She will bring a good bit of money once my buyer gets here. Take your attitude and get out. Don't come back in here until I call for you." Damian's voice was near to shouting as he said the last.

Rachal, cowed and embarrassed to have been made to kneel in the presence of David's newest slut, got up and ran from the room.

Damian turned his attention back to Alice. "Take off the robe." When Alice didn't comply, he moved behind her and snatched it from her shoulders. "When I tell you something do it!" he snarled as he flung the garment to the floor. "I am your Master now and you will obey." He hit his boot with the end of the crop for emphasis.

His free hand took one of the curls which had escaped from the braid the girls had put her hair into after her bath. He ran it through his fingers and brought it to his nose. Her smell was, what, vanilla, and something else, gardenia. Yes, gardenia. He let the hair fall and ran his hand down her back, her sharp intake of breath as he did so was, interesting.

"Alice, David sold you to me and you belong to me. The sooner you understand this" he shrugged, "the better." He guided her to a chair by the desk. "Sit here, I have some questions for you."

Alice sat on the forward three inches of the chair as if she would spring up to runaway. Damian took his seat behind the desk and opened the laptop. Alice held her breath, she hoped Evie had not answered her email, it was not from Alice's IP address but from wherever here was. When Damian did not say anything to her, she began to breathe again.

"Hmm, your new owner will give you the name he wants so I'm not going to change it now. I've got your weight and measurements but there are a couple of things I need to know." He was scrolling through whatever program he was using until he stopped and looked at her. "Any medical problems, ulcers, herpes, STDs, pregnant?" Alice grimaced, "I take that as a no. Medications, anything there? Diabetes meds, depression stuff, birth-control." At the mention of birth-control he noticed how her eyes widened.

"Okay, so birth-control. What kind, pills, IUD, shots." Again, he saw the change in her when he mentioned shots. "Hmm, so that will be ok. Stay in that chair." Damian got up and went to the concealed door. He pushed on it and the lights came on. He stood by the first sink and opened a drawer. Alice couldn't see what he was doing and turned away.

Damian came back in the room and before she knew what was happening, she felt a hypodermic needle pierce her upper arm. "That will take care of the shots. My client will not pay top dollar for a bitch he can't breed."

Alice rubbed her shoulder where the needle went in. She was furious at what he had done and frightened by what he had said. Bitch, breeding, she wasn't a dog! Alice stood up and turned-on Damian.

She didn't see his open hand until it connected to her cheek. Alice's eyes went wide and her look could have burned him down. Damian laughed. "Alice, Alice, Alice, tsk, tsk, tsk. Okay, you don't like that? Well, how about I show you what your alternative would be."

He snapped the chain onto the collar around Alice's neck and pulled her along behind him. The first stop was the bathroom where the labia clips were laying on the cabinet. "Let's just put these back on, I don't like to see my property out without their fine jewelry!"

Damian took her into the corridor and gave her chain a tug. "Walk with me proper. I don't want you marked, but believe me when I tell you, I can hurt you in many ways and there would be no marks. Co-operate and you could have a wonderful life. Your new owner, well if you meet his standards, is wealthier than Midas, and can be very generous. Please him, let him do with you as he wants, bear his babies, and he may let you go when he no longer desires you. Displease him and he can be quite cruel. He might even just send you to one of the brothels in his country where you will spend your short life being fucked by a whole train of men, day and night, until you're all used up."

Alice began to walk with Damian as David had taught her to when on a leash. "That's better, see, it's not that hard is it." He smirked. "Now, let me show you the alternative."

Damian stopped before a door that had a small red light above it. "Let's see what's going on in this room, shall we." Damian quietly opened the door and a man dressed in a suit of clothes that would go well on a CEO of a major corporation, had his fly open and his cock buried in the pussy of the girl on the spanking bench. He was hitting her butt checks with one hand while music played. He was slamming into her and she was screaming. "Scream, bitch, that's right, scream all you want but you will take this and then some." The hand that was not spanking her finally emerged from the area of her clit and a violet wand was arching in it.

Damian backed out and all he said was, "I think that was his secretary." He walked her past other doors, but no lights could be seen. When they came to the stairs, he started down. Alice knew that somewhere down there, her clothes were on a bench along with her jewelry, like her engagement ring and watch. She couldn't remember though, how to find the room, and followed Damian.

Half way down the corridor, he pushed on a panel and a door popped open. "The kennels," was all he said. "This is where Mistress Rachel keeps and trains her subs. The girls who washed you last night are in training and ones who are in formal training or being trained for a client, can be distinguished by the labia clips. In this house, subs do not hide their sex, it is showcased."

A wail could be heard from down the hall and in a room to their left a group of female voices were chanting. Damian made for the room where the screams of a girl could be heard.

It was a large room with bondage tables, a couple of St. Andrew's Crosses were set up, and a long line of chains suspended from the tract in the middle of the ceiling. At each end of the room were small cubicles and in each was a narrow bed.

In the center of the room, suspended by one of the chains, was a girl whose toes barely touched the ground. Her legs were spread open with a spreader-bar that was affixed to the floor. She was in the process of being whipped by a young man in a cock/ball cage but wearing nothing else. Tears were streaming down his face as he flailed away at her.

Mistress Rachel, was taking her frustrations out on the man, urging him on. "You think you're going to get away with diddling one of my girls? You're lucky you still have your cock and balls left!" She yelled. "You whip her good or you're next and I still might turn you into a eunuch."

Damian turned away, "we'll let her deal with her own problems. He moved to the cubicles. "These are the kennels. Each girl sleeps here at night. The ones in formal training have a little bit better arrangement, but still no door and little but a bed and mirror. We don't spoil our subs here. Occasionally we do train subs and even slaves for clients. For them, we have more private arrangements down the hall. When a sub or slave is presented to their owner or a new owner once they leave here, they are of the highest quality. Many times, they are trained to serve all of their Master or Doms special, uhm needs shall we say." He turned to Alice, "so, you can either go quietly and willingly to a new Master, or" he motioned to the kennels, "join us here and spend your time learning to become a sub or slave for the floor or another possible buyer."

Alice looked at him, "floor?"

"Ah, yes, I haven't shown that to you, have I? Well, come then and you will see what our members pay so much to enjoy." He led Alice from the kennels back into the corridor. At the end of the hall was a hidden door that led to another stairs. It was illuminated by soft lights and led up rather sharply. "This is the subs' entry into the main rooms of the club. We have several but as you saw, there were few of them around being idle, yes?"

At the top of the stairs a door opened quietly. Before them was a large room with sofas, chairs, a large table in the middle, and a couple of pool tables. Passageways led off from this room and there were some niches around the room also with small sofas. The room was full of people. Men in tuxes or smart business suits, a few women in evening gowns, but the majority were the subs. And on almost every sofa, the central table, and the pool tables, people were engaged in sex with the subs. Totally naked girls, those who were not yet in training, moved about the room. It was like a scene from a porn movie. It didn't look real and it dawned on Alice, this wasn't real, not like the Master/slave, Dom/sub kind of lifestyle David was training her for. This was solely to satisfy the kinky people that only dabbled in what she would have with David.

David

The interior of the plane was customized to business needs but David wasn't the least bit interested in the décor, he just wanted Alice back. A desk had been setup in the middle of the plane and several chairs surrounded it. David took one of those seats at the urging of Cecil White and he strapped in just as the plane began to move.

One of the gentlemen at the desk looked up from his computer screen. "The subject is still stationary sir."

David looked at Cecil, "explain this," he gestured at the plane and people, "what is going on with my fiancé and where is she? How do we get her back?"

Cecil held up his hand, "back-up there partner, and let me explain. We're all members of Houndsford Security International. Your fiancé's lawyer, very prudently I might add, took out a protection package for Alice Blake when she became twenty-five and came into her inheritance. If she were to be kidnapped, abducted, or otherwise detained, this program would be triggered. An insurance policy is tied to it that would pay a ransom, within reason, to obtain her release. A part of this also included a GPS tracker which, when activated, would give us a location so we could find her."

David shook his head, "I know who has her and why. We need to get to him and get her away from there before something worse happens to her."

"So, maybe it's time you filled me in on just what you know. I don't like my men walking into something blind when they don't have to. I've got some men outside of a location near Boston right now. She is in some kind of a private club. It's looks like a very large estate, has high fences all around it, and a gate that only opens with a pass or something."

David spent the next twenty minutes telling them about the relationship he had with Damian Horace and Rachel Lewis. The confrontation that happened at Master Avery's wake was explained without the addition of any kind of relation to kink and the reason Rachel Lewis was angry with him. "Look, Damian has a beef with me, but why take Alice? She doesn't know anything about this."

"Simple" said Cecil, "hurt you by taking what you obviously care about the most." He turned to the man behind the computer. "Do you still have a fix on her?"

The man nodded in the affirmative and Cecil turned back to David. "We are monitoring her via GPS. She was supplied with a chain and pendant when we took the policy. It's nothing fancy to the naked eye. The chain is gold and so is the pendant. Embedded in the pendant is a single sapphire, it's her birthstone so wouldn't seem out of place, but behind it, in the setting, is the GPS chip. All she had to do was bite down on it and it would activate. Are clients are asked to wear these as a matter of everyday wear, but at least keep them near enough to grab in case of abduction. It doesn't always work out, but in her case it did."

"Usually abductors," he continued, "take off any jewelry or things like that as soon as they can. Alice's GPS didn't go active until she was in the place she is in now, so, we wait to see what happens. If the tracker doesn't move soon, we might be looking at a case where the jewelry was found, but the abductors not knowing it was a tracker, didn't know to destroy it."

"How, uh, how would they destroy it?" David was now worried that Damian had found it or he hadn't but had maybe, oh God no, killed Alice.

"Hold up there a minute. I can see where your mind is going and we're not there yet. Just because she is stationary doesn't mean anything, yet. She maybe drugged or tied up and can't move around."

As bad as any of that sounded it was more hopeful than the dreaded 'D' word. David had to hold onto some hope and that wasn't much but it was something. He looked out at the blankness of the sky. He knew it was getting close to sundown. He should've been standing at the alter getting married soon but now he was speeding through the air at 30,000 feet trying to rescue his love from an ordeal of which he was the cause, at least in Damian's mind. David soon decided that the confines of a plane, no matter how big and fancy, didn't include space for pacing and he needed to do something to take his mind from this before he slipped into madness.

The men around the table kept up a constant communication with the operators on the ground. David tried to be calm but the longer this went on, the worse it was for him. About an hour out from their target, the agent behind the computer whistled. "She's on the move."

Cecil and David crowded behind him and scanned the screen. He enlarged what they were looking at and a tiny blip got bigger and moved ever so slightly around the structure in which it was projected. A Google Maps satellite picture of the estate where Alice was being held was overlayed on the screen to indicate where in the building she was. Another zoom in of the picture and the movement was more pronounced. The information was being relayed to the men on the ground.

Everyone made preparations to take their seats for landing when a notice came from the ground that a limousine with darkened windows was entering the gates to the place where Alice was. The license plates were being forwarded to someone who would check them but there was no way to tell who might be in the car. It turned out the car was from a local hire-car firm who were being questioned about the people who had booked the service. While they waited on the information, the man who was waiting for David and the Houndsford agents at the airport said a private jet had landed and disgorged three men. The three men had gotten into the limo and sped away. The plane's tail number was being traced and it was found no flight-plan had been filed, either inbound or for an outbound departure.

By the time they were on the ground, there was more information on the plane. It was owned by a series of shell-companies which would take time to unravel. In the meantime, and with an abundance of caution, Cecil put a couple of men on the lookout for who might return to that plane. The Houndsford plane was parked near enough to it that for the suspicious jet to leave, it had to pass their plane.

Alice

Alice was not an exhibitionist and the party and collaring renewal ceremony she had attended and worn the robe of a sub/slave at least still left her with the sense of being covered. Dressed or more factually undressed as she was with the labia clips and red coloring highlighting her clit the way it did, was more than Alice could handle. She was revulsed and the idea of being so publicly displayed made her sick with waves of nausea. When Damian pulled the chain that was attached to the collar around her neck she balked and dug her high-heels in.

"I'm warning you Alice," he snarled, "either you comply or this," he gestured around the room, "will be your life. If you're lucky, I might find you another buyer or you could find someone here who wants you for his own private sub or slave." He chuckled, "of course, the longer you're here, the more familiar you become to everyone, and you'll just be like any of the others, nothing more than something akin to a piece of furniture to be used, abused, or fucked as a member might desire."

"Let me show you what other kinds of things go on here, it might help you decide if staying is what you want or if you would prefer the ownership of just one Master." When Damian pulled the chain again Alice took a step forward. Damian stopped at a table near the main floor and picked up a simple eye-mask. He put it on Alice before taking her out onto the floor. "I don't want anyone seeing you before the sale." He whispered in her ear.

More than a few people stopped and stared at the submissive Master Damian was leading across the floor. He paused a couple of times to address direct questions about Alice but in each instance stressed she was not available and in one case, not for sale. At the far side of the room, a set of double doors was guarded by two men dressed as gladiators. "This area is only for select members," was all Damian said.

The doors were opened and another long corridor lay ahead but to the right was a large room. It looked like a study from an older, statelier home. Oak paneled, a large hearth with a roaring fire, and expensive Persian-carpets. Chairs and sofas graced the room with a curious grouping in front of the fireplace.

The furniture before the fireplace was a half-circle of wing-backed chairs around a large ottoman. On it was a naked woman with a man with his cock in her mouth and another with his cock in her ass. A third man was using a gally whip on her back. The chairs were all filled by men and one woman watching what was happening to the one being abused. The men were having their cocks serviced by the mouth of a sub and for the woman, her legs were splayed open and a young man was licking her clit while she pulled at her own nipples. In other parts of the room two and sometimes three people were engaging in sex and the at center of each group was a sub, some dressed as Alice but in other cases, subs who were totally naked.

Further down the hallway, a room with a red light above it was the next stop on this walk of horrors. Alice could hear the screams before the door even opened. A glance inside showed a sub, handcuffed to two posts, being whipped by a woman in the leather accouterments of a Dominatrix.

Before they could go into the room a vibration of a phone was heard coming from Damian's jacket pocket. He quietly closed the door and the screams of the girl were muffled again. "What?" Damian said, listening. He turned to Alice with a big smile on his face. "Excellent, excellent, we will be right there. Yes, she is with me. Momentarily." He cut the call and put the phone in his pocket.

Turning to Alice, "it seems your new Master is here and he is eager to see you. I'm going to leave you for a few minutes so I can talk a bit a business with him and you can get freshened up before you meet him. Come this way." He pulled her chain and Alice dutifully followed. Up the stairs again and down the hall. He stopped before the doors to his office and opened a door to the room next to it. "Now, you go in there and I'll be in to get you. There is a bathroom in there and you do what you need to." He pulled the chain so hard, Alice stumbled into him but then righted herself. "Careful, Careful! we don't want you hurt."

Alice whispered something then went into the room and he closed and locked the door. Alice had fallen against him for a reason and it was in her hands. She had Damian's phone. Alice prayed she could call David before it was too late.

With shaking hands, she fumbled with the phone, almost dropping it. After a couple of deep breaths, she got her nerves under control. Fortunately, the phone was not locked and she dialed David's number. One ring, two rings, God where was he, did he really sell her, three rings, please, please it can't be true, "hello" it was David's voice, "who is this and what do you want?" he said forcefully.

"David," she said hesitantly, "David, it's me, Alice." She heard the shout on the other end of the phone. "David, why did you sell me?"

Another voice, unrecognizable, was now on the phone, a more matter of fact voice. "Miss Blake, this is Cecil White. I'm with Houndsford "

Before he could finish, she cut in, "look, shut up and listen, I'm about to be sold to some guy as a breeder just like a dog. Come and get me!"

"We're almost to you. Keep this line open so we can hear what goes on and we can track your signal. Can you do that?"

"Yes, but hurry!" She put the phone in her cincher, in the back. Next, she took her hair down and looking in the bathroom, found a brush and brushed it out. The hair hung down on her back far enough it would help hide the phone. Now, all she could do was wait, wait for David to rescue her or to be sold like some animal in the market.

Alice heard the key turn in the lock and Damian strode in. "Alice, get in here." He clipped the chain back on her collar and noticed her hair down. "Didn't like the hairdo the girls gave you huh. It's okay, your hair does look nice down. Your new owner likes long hair, gives him something to grab onto when he fucks you." He chuckled at that last.

He led Alice out of the room and into his office. Two large men stood at the door as guards. The man sitting next to the sofa must be the buyer, Alice thought.

Damian walked her up to him and he told her to kneel but the man waved him away. "Turn." The man said and Alice turned around until she was facing him again. "Hmm, I like the hair, her eyes are interesting, and the body is good."

He stood. Alice thought he might be in his sixties, tall and not fat. His suit probably cost more than some cars and was definitely wearing a bespoke suit, tailored to his body and tastes. He had long, manicured fingers that looked as if he had never done any manual labor in his life beyond picking up a fork or a cup of coffee. He looked at Alice with intense dark eyes and she noticed his full head of dark brown hair curled around on itself in a curious cut for a man. Perhaps because he was used to wearing a hat but then Alice really didn't want to have to find that out firsthand.

"Speak girl, tell me your first name." The man said.

"Alice," she said, "my name is Alice."

Turning to Damian, "has she ever been married, children?"

"No, no children and never been married." Damian told him, wishing he would finish this so they could close the deal.

"Hmph, take her to the restroom and have her take that bunch of clips off and clean up that stuff you've put on her clit. You've painted her up like a clown! Put her in something so I can take her with me. I don't want anyone else looking at my property," he said as he turned toward Damian.

Alice began to move toward the bathroom concealed behind the door near the sofa. Damian stopped her and unclipped the chain from her neck. "There should be a dress on a hook behind the door." Turning back to the visitor. "So, are you ready to make a deal?"

Alice pushed on the panel which concealed the bathroom and breathed a sigh of relief that the phone had not been found but now what, should she take off the cincher because if she did, where would she put the phone? She left the door to the bathroom open and tried to listen to what was being said but couldn't hear anything.

On the back of the door was a plain dress with buttons down the front made from a loose woven cotton. It was soft, but she knew it would chafe against her bare skin, especially the more sensitive parts like her nipples. She removed the clips and took a wet wash cloth to try removing the red stuff they'd painted her clit with but it wouldn't budge. A bit of soap fixed that and she buttoned the dress over the cincher.

"Come here Alice," it was the voice of Damian. "It's time for you to greet your new Master." She heard him laugh at that last statement. He might find this funny, but she didn't.

Leaving the bathroom, she saw the two men shaking hands. When she came to stand before the man who thought he had bought her, she opened her mouth to speak but Damian slapped her, hard. "You don't speak until your Master gives you permission, understood?"

Alice nodded. Damian looked at the buyer, "are you sure you don't want to take the time to sample this new one. I can give you one of my best rooms for the night and anything you want to let you take your ease here, you only have to ask."

The man shook his head. "No, I have someplace to be and I have everything I need on the plane." He pulled a silver chain from his pocket and snapped it on Alice's collar. "I will return this collar to you the next time I come here. It will do for now though." He looked at Alice, "hmm, I don't like the name Alice, I shall give you a new name, but now you will just be my pet." He gave the chain a slight tug, "come pet, I need to be gone from here."

David, Cecil, and …

David was beside himself with worry. The phone call chilled him to his very core when he heard the fright and anguish in Alice's voice. How could she believe he thought so little of her to believe he had sold her? Sitting in the back of the SUV with Cecil and two other men, he was close to despair.

One of the men, had connected a recording device to David's phone so everything that could be heard on the phone would be kept to use in a prosecution of the people responsible for the abduction of their client. Houndsford had a crack legal team on the payroll that was particular about such things and this recording would be the icing on their prosecution case.

Marty, the man who did the computer work on the Houndsford plane had cracked the ownership of the jet and found it belonged to a holding company which was totally owned by one very rich, powerful, and notorious former arms-dealer who had supplied wars and revolutions in the Middle East, Africa, and Latin America making himself an obscene fortune along the way. His current permanent residence was a private island off the coast of Panama which he owned and that could only be accessed by boat, seaplane, or helicopter.

As the SUV skidded to a stop at their destination, Cecil and the two men with him hopped out of the car as a limousine was caught half in and half out of the large gates to the estate where The Arabesque club was located. An identical SUV to the one David was in was blocking the front of the car and two men with drawn guns were at the back to keep the driver from reversing back into the private grounds. Two men with guns drawn exited the limo and guarded the back doors.

Cecil went up to one of them and talked. He might as well have been talking to a tree. No response, but when he started to reach for the door handle, the gun came around and leveled on Cecil's head. Cecil's men took exception to their boss's dilemma. Two put their guns on the man who was pointing a gun at Cecil and two others, from the men who had been watching the club, did the same with the man's companion on the other side of the car.

David exited the SUV. The back window of the limo on Cecil's side opened a couple of inches. Cecil got a glimpse of Alice, cowering in the corner and could see the profile of a man he thought he recognized from pictures taken long ago. The man began to speak, demanding he be allowed to continue his journey. Cecil cut him off and told him he was here to get his protectee, Alice Blake. The window went back up, the conversation was over.

Cecil went to where David was standing by the SUV he had ridden in from the airport. "I think I recognize that guy." Cecil said as he ducked back into the car. Pulling out his phone he punched in a number and waited for the answer. "Hey, I think maybe the guy you're looking for on the shell-company may be our old buddy Amin Jaffar," He listened, "yep, he's aged but that's him. We chassed his ass from Bagdad to Kabul and never got him. I could describe him to you in my sleep." He waited while the man on the other end supplied him with more information. "Okay, give them a call and we'll hold here, but our primary concern is to get the girl back," again, he listened, "yep, had eyes on her, but can't get to her. Short of a gun fight with his guards, it will have to be a standoff. If they want him, tell them to get their asses over here."

David heard the name and recognized it from some of the stories his Uncle Maurice used to tell him about Beirut. He went to the car where Alice was being held prisoner and said something to one of the guards in a foreign language. This time, there was a reaction. The man looked at him and carefully removed his sunglasses. Eye to eye, David continued to talk to the man. He lowered his weapon, turned, and tapped on the window. It slid down a bit and the guard leaned in and talked to his employer.

The guard stood and motioned David to talk to the man in the car. The window went half way down and David leaned down to see Alice, wide-eyed with fright, cowering in the fetal position in the far corner of the car. He turned his attention to the man holding a silver chain that was clipped to his love's neck. Without speaking the man pulled the chain and forced Alice to come to his side.

The two men talked in Jaffar's native language. David explained who he was, his relationship to Alice, and the problem that Damian believed he had with David. Jaffar listened then turned to David and told him it was not his problem what his pet had been to him, she was his now and would be leaving with him, "I've become quite attached to her, I bought her, she's mine, it is what it is." He started to raise the window when another group of SUVs took up positions in front of the gates. More armed men piled out and surrounded the limo. These men didn't just have handguns, but military assault equipment normally found on the battlefield.

Jaffar closed the window and David turned to find a slightly shorter, older, but solidly built man in a tailored suit striding toward him. He put out his hand and said his name was John. "Son, we can take this from here. Cecil tells me your fiancé might be in this car."

David nodded, "she was kidnapped."

John looked surprised, "Jaffar kidnapped her? Never knew he was into that!"

"No, no," David was saying, "he didn't kidnap her, Damian Horace did it. He has some crazy beef with me, said I owed him a life, and he took her on our wedding day. We were supposed to be married last night, uh, yesterday."

"So, where is this Damian and how does Jaffar have her?" John queried.

"Damian is in there," David said pointing down the lane to where the estate was, "It's a private club called The Arabesque. He took Alice there and sold her to this guy. I just want her back."

John looked at David. He could see the anguish in his face and the way his eyes were glistening, he could tell this man was just barely holding it together. John squeezed David's shoulder. "Look, I'll get your girl back but you might want to take her away before the rest of the people get here. Understand?" David nodded his agreement.

The driver, terrified of what was happening around his car, unlocked the doors of the limo. The men pulled both Jaffar and Alice out of the back. David took Alice and Cecil took them both to the SUV the Houndsford men had arrived in. In the back seat, David wrapped Alice in a blanket and sat her on his lap. They sped off to the airport where the plane was waiting to take them home. As they were speeding down the exit road, more SUVs were going toward the club.

On the plane, the computer tech, Marty, was transferring the audio files of the open phone line to an interested federal agency. Another man was starting the file on the operation itself. The only thing they would need is Alice's narrative of what had happened. One of the members of the team was licensed to take legal testimony from a witness/victim.

What Alice would say about the ordeal would most likely be used in a case against her abductor and anyone else involved in the crime.

When the plane took off David ignored the "please fasten your seat belts" as he held Alice on his lap. He had failed to protect her, something Maurice had drummed into him from the very start, loyalty, honor, and protection of the family, were part of who David had been raised to be. As he stroked Alice's hair, the tears began to fall from David as the enormity of what had just happened finally caught up to him.

One of the team on the plane, a group that seem to have grown since they'd initially arrived in Boston, approached David. "Here, let me take her. She's in shock, and needs care." Absently, David finally looked up at him,

"But, I'm a doctor you see, I have to take care of her, it's my duty to do that …" he trailed off. The tears from his eyes continued to flow.

"Sir, I'm sure you are a great doctor, but you are too close to her to take care of her right now and from the looks of it, you're in a bit of shock yourself." Gently he picked up Alice, "I'm a trained medic and have delt with shock on the battlefield. Let me look after the two of you."

The man laid Alice on one of the sofas in the back of the plane and then led David to the one opposite. He covered David and put an inflatable cushion under his feet before returning to Alice. He did the same for her and then sat between the two and took temps, blood pressure, and other vitals. An ambulance would be waiting for them when they touched down. Until then, he monitored their condition.

David began pulling out of it after about an hour. His adrenalin levels were coming back to normal and he sat up, drank a bottle of water fortified with electrolytes, and asked to speak to Cecil.

"Look, uh, I need to get a phone call off to my dad to let him know we are okay."

Cecil smiled, "he has already been told, but I imagine your mom would like to hear your voice." He pulled a sat-phone from his jacket pocket and handed it to David. "Don't worry, it's secure, scrambled, so you don't need to think anybody is listening in on a private conversation."

Gratefully, David took the phone, dialed his parent's home phone and talked to his parents. His mother began to tell him what she had done about the wedding but David brushed that off, "I need to take care of her now, mom, the wedding can come later. If we have to, I'll take her to Vegas and get married." He listened for a few more minutes and assured her he would let them be at any wedding he had. "Yah, okay, I'll call you when I know. I love you mom, more than you know." He hung up while his mom cried happy tears.

David reached over and took Alice's hand. Ever so slightly she turned her head and looked at him but he wasn't sure she was really seeing him. "My sweet, you have to believe I never wanted anything like this to happen to you. Damian is a pig and so is Rachel. Please believe me, I didn't sell you, you can't be sold, you belong to me. You know …" Alice broke off his declaration when she turned her head back and closed her eyes. David was shattered by the vacant look she had given him.

Where is Alice?

The Houndsford plane disembarked its passengers at the local airport and an ambulance was waiting to take Alice and David to the hospital. The staff at the hospital was surprised to find David and his bride in the ER. David had called from the ambulance and talked to a friend who was to meet them there.

Dr. Jason Wagner was a short, older man who had been David's friend for years. He was a kink-friendly man who was a member of the same group of Masters and Doms to which David belonged. He knew the collaring had been canceled but hadn't been told the reason. As he stood with David next to the bed where Alice was lying, he was told the most frightful and horrible of reasons why.

"We had to cancel the wedding and of course the collaring. This guy had taken her to a place outside of Boston." David was telling his friend. "My god, he sold her! Who does that!"

Dr. Wagner could hear the panic in David's voice but had him sit while he checked over Alice. He had a soothing voice and started by trying to reassure the girl she was safe. He decided a sedative was in order and when the nurse brought it, he was the one to administer the drug. He smoothed the hair off her face and quietly told her he would take care of her until she drifted off to sleep.

She was taken to a room and David went in with her. He lovingly undressed her and put a gown on her so she could sleep. A cot was brought in so he could stay with her. His friend had tried to get him to be admitted but he refused to leave Alice's side. Dr. Wagner relented and slipped him a bit of a sedative in his tea. David needed his sleep too.

Alice was screaming! David sat bolt upright, trying to get his bearings. The hospital room came into focus and Alice's second scream brought him to her bed to comfort her. She was still sleeping and fought his embrace. Nurses came in as he tried to comfort her. Finally, her eyes started to flutter open and she saw it was David who held her and not the man who had so casually bought her from Damian.

David stepped back to let the nurses check her vitals and generally make sure it was not David who had set her off. One of the nurses asked him to come out into the hall. "Dr. Khoury, can you tell me what that was?"

"Nurse, uh, she is my fiancé, we were supposed to be married this past Saturday but she was abducted. A group of security professionals and I rescued her and she has been in shock. She was screaming in her sleep. I, was trying to comfort her, let her feel safe." He said while running his hands through his hair in frustration at being pulled away from his girl.

"Doctor, I think what she needs is some professional guidance. In military people they call it PTSD, and she is showing some signs of it. Does she had a therapist she might relate to or feel comfortable with?"

David's first thought was of Master Morris, Alice had seemed comfortable with him and he would understand more than any other therapist about what her trauma might be. "I think I have just the person," he looked at the nurse, "thank you for your suggestion, I'll get on it as soon as I can."

"Excellent, sleep well. Dr. Wagner left an order for a light sedative which we have given to her so she will sleep for a few more hours. I think she needs it, don't you?"

"Thank you nurse, I'll get back to Alice," he said, "good night."

When David entered the room again, a young nurse was just finishing up taking care of Alice. He could tell by the way she was breathing that Alice had again fallen asleep. He only wished he could take away the horror that he had inflicted upon her, even if it was through Damian, he was still the one it had emanated from.

Damian had been his roommate from the first day of med-school. The housing had been a blessing because he didn't want to have to maintain an apartment in Boston and wasn't sure where he would get into a residency program. Damian just seemed a good fit for him.

They were probably two weeks into the program when Damian had invited him to go with him to a members' only club located in a quiet part of the city. David didn't have much else to do that night, homework was caught up, and he wasn't behind in anything. So, they went.

The place was called The Arabesque. Damian's father, the senior member of a very old money family, had been a member in his younger days and had given it over to his son when he turned twenty-one. David had never given Damian any indication that he was into BDSM or even had the proclivity.

What David saw that night had really opened his eyes about some of the kink people would get up to even as role-play. For David, he was really more along the lines of Uncle Maurice, the Doms and Masters of the group his uncle belonged to and the ones he had been sent to in Boston at his uncle's urging. What he saw that night was mind-blowing.

The house itself was set back from the street. It was enclosed by a high wall and a gate that only opened from orders coming from inside the club. A valet opened car doors and membership was checked at the door before entry. It was a very large house and the people within were expecting others to respect their privacy.

Damian had cautioned David about privacy on the drive over. He had two eye-masks that would cover the upper part of their head and recommended they put them on. "If you recognize anyone in there or ever see them on the street, ever," he stressed, "you don't know them, never seen them, and they have never seen you. This place is dedicated to keeping their clients kink-life secret."

The man checked Damian's membership and they were waved into the club with a "welcome, gentlemen, have a memorable night," from the guard.

The foyer soared two stories and a huge light-sculpture hung from the ceiling to diffuse light in hundreds of rays. In the room to the right, quiet mummers were heard mixed with an occasional laugh. Inside the room, men and women were sitting on sofas, chairs, and in some cases on tables. They were others who were milling about, speaking in low tones. Among them, girls dressed in collars, black lace bustiers that hid nothing, stockings with garter belts, six-inch heals, and nothing to cover their genitals. The girls were also wearing chains attached to their collars which were held by some of the men. Those who's chains had not been claimed, were held in the girl's own hands, signifying they were available.

Damian walked past that room and into another, larger room at the end of the corridor. A couple of large tables, several groupings around the room of sofas and chairs, some with ottomans at their center and others with a bench, was about half filled with mostly men but some women.

David noticed that all of the people, except for the girls being led by chains, wore masks. Some were only eye-masks like the ones he and Damian wore and other were full-face masks to hide the wearers' identity completely. Here, there were more girls dressed like the ones in the first room and most were on leashes. There were a couple, stripped bare, who were restrained on a bench or over an ottoman, each one was being fucked by a man in a suit, mask, and with only his cock out of his pants so he could take his pleasure. There was more than one man holding the leash of a sub, who had his cock out and the girl was on her knees in front of him with his cock in her mouth.

Damian still did not stop but continued on. Behind a curtain at the far end of the room was another hallway at the end of which was a staircase going down. Along this hallway the dark walls were broken up by small alcoves where small sofas were tucked away but from the ceiling in each hung a chain. In two of them a naked woman was displayed with a man or men sitting on the sofa fucking a woman or women.

David was no prude and he had seen a Master fuck his slave in public or share her with another Master to fuck in public, but these were all within the confines of a private dungeon. The purpose of these actions was manyfold, but David had never considered he would ever want to do that, for himself, or one he owned. Damian, however was drinking in the sights but continued to the stairs in front of them.

As they descended, Damian turned slightly and said, "now you get to see the dungeons."

"Wait, wait, just hold up. What gives you the idea I'm even interested in this place or a dungeon tour?" he asked Damian. "Why do you even have me here."

Damian just laughed. "Do you really think I don't know about you and that group of Masters and Doms you hang out with a couple of times a month? I have it on good authority that you are just as kinky as I am. Don't you think I had you checked out before I agreed to roommate with you?"

David had nothing to say to that except, "it's private and it should stay that way. I don't know where you get your information from but don't broadcast it." The two continued down the stairs. Finally, they stopped at a door and without hesitation, Damian entered and bid David follow him. Damian held his finger to his lips to make sure David didn't make any noise that would disturb the scene in front of them.

In the center of the room were two pillars. Between the pillars was a girl in a black waist-cincher, black stockings and stiletto heels. Her hands were bound out-stretched and her legs also opened and bound to the same pillars. A dominatrix and a man in a suit stood with whips while another older man with greying hair, sat in a chair. David and Damian moved to stand in the shadows.

The man with the whip was being egged on by the dominatrix to be more forceful in the lashes he was administering but each time she felt he hadn't given all he could she supplemented his efforts with her own whip. Finally, the man began to get it right in the eyes of the dominatrix. The girl between the pillars screamed several times, but no one stopped. Sweat pouring down his brow, the man finally dropped the whip and looked at the back of the girl. His sobs could be heard almost as loudly as the girl who had been whipped. Turning to the man in the chair, the dominatrix looked to him. With a nod, she picked up the whip and left through a side door.

The old man stood, "son, get that bitch wife of yours down from there and clean her up. Maybe she'll learn she can't spread her legs for every man in town." He turned away and Damian touched David on the arm. He nodded toward the door and they left.

"Shit, man," Damian said in a whisper, "God, imagine doing that to your wife! Course, too bad my old man doesn't have the nuts to do that to the slut he's married to. She's spread so thin around town I'm not surprised she's not pregnant again. Now I even wonder if the two kids she's given dad are his or somebody else's." Damian stopped, "you know, I'm going to ask dad about that the next time I see him. I'll tell him they have a 'keep you wife's legs closed' cure right here. Course, she wouldn't make it past the first wallop of a whip." Damian smiled with that and seemed pleased with himself. David should have known then he was a dangerous person.

Damian and David continued to share quarters until the end of the second semester. Since the trip to The Arabesque, David and Damian had never talked about it and Damian had never invited David back. A couple of times, when David was going to meet with the local Dom/Master's group he was involved with, Damian had hinted about going with him, but David never offered.

A week before the final exams, David had finished an essay that one of the professors had asked to be included with each of the student's final submissions for the course. David sent his in electronically in the early hours of one morning when he had just finished it. Two days later, Damian printed out the same essay, with changes to authorship, and handed it in to the same professor. Dr. Levitt called David and Damian into his office the next day. Before the day was over, Damian was moved out of graduate-student housing and was gone. David hadn't seen nor heard from Damian until Master Avery's wake.

David woke fitfully. Daylight streamed through the window in Alice's hospital room. A nurse was at her side taking a blood sample, then handed it to the tech who was waiting to take it to the lab. The machines connected to his love were all beeping and humming along normally. Nothing to be alarmed about. As the nurse left, she smiled at the Doctor on the cot.

He pulled his cellphone from the table next to him to catch the time. Nine-forty, okay he could deal with that. A tray of uneaten breakfast was on an adjustable tray-table at the end of Alice's bed. He lifted the lid and grimaced. If it ever had been edible, it wasn't now.

David put his shoes on and headed to the bathroom. When he came out, he went to stand by Alice's bed. A familiar voice could be heard in the hall. He stepped out and Jason Wagner was holding Alice's chart and talking to the nurse. He saw David and held up a finger to wait.

The doctor and nurse finished then Dr. Wagner turned to David. "So, how are you feeling this morning? Sleep well?"

David ran his hands through his hair, a familiar nervous reaction he had, "I'm doing okay Jason, it's Alice I worry about."

His friend patted his shoulder, "she's okay, well basically. She is still in some shock, but that is to be expected, from what you told me, it must have been like a trip through hell. Some people, well most people actually, have no idea what life in a dedicated Master/slave or even Dom/sub relationship is like. Sure, role-playing is good and many times you see people who session in a dungeon doing more role-playing than something that is satisfying a need. I don't think my girl and I have ever played outside of a private dungeon and then only on special occasions like my collaring her or a renewal ceremony."

"I know you had to postpone both your wedding and collaring, I get that, but right now, your girl is my patient and I don't think she is near ready for anything that intense. Give her time, have her talk with a therapist." Jason said softly to David.

"I know, she needs someone to talk to and I think I'll call Master Morris and see if he will take her on. Or, at least tell me someone who knows us to help her." David's brow was still creased with worry. "When can I take her home?"

Jason Wagner turned to face David, "I certainly want to keep her another twenty-four hours. David, she may not want to go home with you. Don't you see, this is a trauma that might need more than a few sedatives and a talk to a therapist to solve. She has to want to go home, want to be with you, and want to be over this. She will always remember what happened, but she needs to be able to deal with what happened. Give her that time or you might never get her back to the health, mental health, she had before."

David's head sagged. "Okay, let me call Master Morris and see what I can get worked out. Thank you, buddy, thank you."

David turned to go back into Alice's room when he saw Evie and Amara coming off the elevator. He waited for them in the hall. "Oh David, please tell me she's okay!" Evie pleaded. "I feel so bad about what happened and we were so scared for her." By the looks of her, she had been crying and Amara, had a good grip on her arm in case she needed him.

"She's still under sedation and will be here for at least another twenty-four hours. I just talked to her doctor and he said that physically she checks out, but he is worried about the trauma. I'm calling a friend who I hope will do some therapy with her." David led them into the room so Evie could sit with her friend.

When Evie saw the cot, she told David that she wanted to sit with her friend for a while and if he wanted to go freshen up and make his calls, she would stay until he got back.

David went to the doctor's lounge where he had a locker with shower items, shaving kit, and change of clothes. While he undressed, he called Master Morris and gave him an overview of what happened to Alice and the fact she would need someone to talk to about the trauma. Jon Morris agreed to meet him at the hospital in an hour.

Shaved, showered, changed, and having had coffee and a roll, David was ready to greet Jon Morris. When David got back to Alice's room, he found Cecil White and his cousin George standing just outside her door.

Cecil turned to David, "your cousin George has filled me in on the local situation. I really do need to speak to Alice, but when you have a few minutes, I need to have you give me your statement. Nothing fancy," he stressed," just enough for the lawyers." He motioned to the closed door, "I take it she's not quite up to answering any questions?" he asked. "I understand about the shock, but we do need a statement."

"I get that," David said, "I've got an old friend, a therapist, who's going to look at her, I mean, she's not even awake yet." He looked through the small window in the door, "let me find out something and I'll call you."

Cecil was not budging and neither was George. "Look, there is stuff you need to tell me before I can say anything about what has been happening."

"Okay, come here." David led them to an empty consulting room and turned to look at them. "What do you want to know beyond what I've already told you?"

George started but Cecil held up his hand, "let me" he said to George. Turning to David. "Who is Damian and Rachal to you and how does all of this tie into Amin Jaffar? This is one fucked up bunch of shit this girl has been through. She was my protectee and as soon as that GPS tweerped, she became my responsibility."

David had not had the right amount of sleep in the last few days and neither were his nerves not on a hair-fire trigger. "She was, is, and always will be my responsibility! Now if you'll just shut the fuck up and sit down," looking at his cousin George, "and you, sit and chill."

Cecil could understand where all of this was coming from but still bristled until he figured he needed to give the man time to talk. And talk he did. David related the Hallmark version of his connection to Damian and Rachal. "… for some reason, she had the hots for me and the guy she was with got pissed. He put her and her junk out in the street and told her to go. Rachel expected me to take her in and deal with her shit. I was in med-school and didn't even live off campus but in university graduate housing."

George kept his mouth shut but not Cecil, "so you hadn't seen him until this wake?"

"Hadn't seen him. His dad was a big doner to the university and they didn't want to make a huge deal out of this guy's kid getting sent down for cheating, plagiarism if you will, so they, very quietly, switched him out of the med-school program and into another one. The next I even heard of him was when Avery had called me to Boston when he was dying. There was some stuff he wanted me to do and then he told me Rachel Lewis was with Damian Horace and that Damian's dad had died, left him a pile of money, and he bought The Arabesque. The estate where we found Alice was the old Horace estate. He'd moved the club to his own property. Probably as a thumb in the eye to his father."

"Hmm, well, surveillance video taken at the estate confirms a lot of this. I have to tell you, a great deal of what I saw there made me sick. I did three tours in Afghanistan before I switched over to Houndsford, and all the shit I saw there didn't make me half as sick as that club video." He took out a notebook and looked at something. "The local police, along with the FBI, found three girls under eighteen, that's underage in Massachusetts, working in that club and living in something they called the 'kennels.' Geez, inspection of Damian Horace's computer revealed his sale of more than ten women in the last three years and the purchase of six in that same time period. We also found the bank accounts he was using to shift money around trying to hide his trafficking operations. He and Miss Lewis are in custody. The, uh, members who were in attendance were not detained."

"I, uh, want to know if," David was having a hard time getting the words out, "was there anything with Alice on the tapes, the surveillance tapes?"

Cecil leaned over and patted David's arm, "sir, we found nothing that even shows she had been there except the money transfer from Amin Jaffar and Damian Horace. Supposedly for 'services rendered.' Her image is nowhere to be found except for a New York Times notice of your impending nuptials and a picture, head shot, of Miss Blake."

David looked at his cousin who nodded his head. "We still need to talk to Alice, but it can wait," George looked at Cecil, "right Mr. White, we can talk to her tomorrow. We'll go and let you get back to her."

The three left the consulting room together. Just exiting the elevator were a woman and two men dressed in dark suits, white shirts, and for the men, ties. The sunglasses they all wore covered any chance of checking their eyes for a threat. Cecil White stood by Alice's door and as the three approached, he acted as a block against anyone entering.

The woman removed her sunglass and as if on cue, so did the two men behind her. Each one pulled out a badge and credentials that had FBI boldly printed on them. "My name is Janice Walker, FBI, special agent, and I'm here to talk to Miss Alice Blake." Looking at Cecil, "and you are?" she questioned.

"Cecil White, Houndsford Security International, how can I help you, SP Walker?" Cecil said as he also flashed his ID. David and his cousin George, took places beside Cecil.

Softening her tone a bit, the woman from the FBI said, "I'm here to speak to Alice Blake. The Damian Horace affair is being investigated for kidnapping and taking an abductee across state lines, a federal offence. We are here to get her statement. Can I please speak to her?"

"Miss Blake is here because of the shock she suffered and is still being sedated. I also need to talk to her as does Detective", he motioned to David's cousin, "George Khoury of the Green Valley PD."

David stepped forward, "and I'm her fiancé, Dr. David Khoury. We were supposed to be married the day of her abduction so you can imagine, we can be very protective of her."

"Humph, well, we need to get her side of the story." David opened his mouth to say something, "and before you ask, no I can't tell you anything about what's going on because we need statements from each of you without any info you might get from us tainting your testimony." She looked at the door we had just come out of, signaling toward it with her hand, "Is she in there?"

"No, I'm a doctor on staff here and that is a vacant consulting room. We just use it when we need to talk or take out conversations out of the hallway." Pointing at Alices room, "my fiancé is in here. We can go in the consulting room, if you like."

Without a word Agent Walker pushed her way into the consulting room. The two agents with her took positions on either side of the door to Alice's room. Agent Walker asked Cecil White to join her for, "a chat."

David saw Master Morris step out of the elevator and head his way. David excused himself from cousin George and went to meet his friend before he got to the FBI men standing outside Alice's room. He took Jon Morris to a waiting room and they sat in the corner where no one could hear. David related what had happened to Alice, the abduction, rescue, and now the investigation. "Believe me, she was in deep shock and is still sedated. Dr. Wagner, Master Jason, is looking after her. Now the FBI and everyone else wants to question her. I don't know what happened to her, but I can guess."

While Jon Morris listened intently but asking clarifying questions when needed, David recounted how he knew Damian Horace, the one trip he had made to The Arabesque under the previous owners, and the expelling of Damian from med-school. "He blames me and took Alice as a revenge payment for what he thought I *owed* him." David said with a pained look in his eyes, "and then he *sold* her as a sex slave/breeder to some guy, Amin Jaffar to be exact." Tears were just about to spill from David's eyes.

Jon put an arm around David's shoulders. "Okay, I think I can help, but I need to see Alice, even if she is still sleeping, I need to see her." Turning to David, "and I think you and I need to do some talking, too. This has affected you and don't think you can just skate away from it. But right now, take me to Alice."

David and Jon Morris left the room and headed for the door guarded by the two men who had come in with Agent Walker. David pointed at Jon Morris and simply said "doctor" as the men looked them over. One of the guards pushed open the door as he stepped aside.

David looked at his sleeping sweetheart. He hair spread across the pillow and framed her face so beautifully it was hard to think of what she had seen or been subjected to during the whole ordeal. She had been thoroughly examined, physically, when she was first brought in and there had been no signs she had been molested, but what had they done to her mind? This and a myriad of other horrors plagued David's mind and imagination.

Jon Morris looked at the chart that was kept at the end of Alice's bed and then he looked at Alice. He saw the same girl whom David had brought to his home in the days following her rejection by David's family. She was a strong person; he could see that in her when they spoke. But she was also naïve when it came to the kind of people and things, he could only imagine she had witnessed.

He had seen clubs like The Arabesque himself. Most were well run, respectable establishments with world-class cliental, but what David had told him impressed him as being not much more than a kinky whore house, albeit one where the men wore tuxes, their women were arrayed in long dresses, and the girls in little more than stockings and high-heels. From the interactions Jon Morris had with Alice in the past, such things could well have been too much for her to handle. If she had been put in a situation where her body would have been valued as nothing more than meat for sale in a market, it might well have been a full-blown break, He would have to see her first to find out what had happened and then how to try to allow her to deal with it in a meaningful way.

Lying in the hospital bed, she looked like the picture of young-womanhood. He could see why David was so enthralled with her and was so patient in her training. The beautiful hair splayed over the pillow as she slept, the uncreased brow, and the serene look on her face showed she was not in distress in her sleep. How would she be when awake? It was hard to say but David had told him about the screams in her sleep the night before and need for a further tranquilizer to ease her back to Morpheus.

A nurse came into Alice's room and Jon asked her about the last dose of tranquilizer. "It was given at 3:20 am. She should be waking up soon. You must be the therapist Dr. Khoury mentioned last night," the nurse said.

"Jon Morris, PhD. and yes, I'm going to be her therapist. Thank you for the information, I think I'll just sit with her for a bit in case she does wakeup." Jon took a seat by the bed and David sat on Alice's other side. Jon wanted to be there when she did wake because he wanted to see what her reaction was to David. How he would treat her would depend a lot on how that turned out.

Cecil White stuck his head in and motioned for David to come. "She," motioning with his head toward the room where Agent Walker was doing interviews, "wants to see you and the therapist. She's seen me and your cousin so we are going to go get some breakfast then maybe comeback and see if Alice can talk yet. You and I need to sit down about her continued safety when you get a few minutes."

David left Alice with Jon and went in to give his statement to Agent Walker. For the next twenty minutes he told Agent Walker everything he knew about Damian Horace and Rachel Lewis. He answered all of her questions and left nothing out. David had expected that all of this information would result in some info being shared with him about what the FBI had found and what they were going to do about Damian and Rachel, but all he got was a 'we'll be in touch' from the agent.

Alice was still not awake when he slid, once again, into the chair by her bed. Jon Morris was reading something on the tablet he'd brought with him and except for the sounds of the machines in the room, all was quiet. David saw it first. He'd watched Alice sleep in his arms as he held her several times since they first became intimate in Florence. Her eyelids began to flutter and her breathing changed. Jon Morris put down the tablet and moved closer to the bed. He wanted to observe this first interaction between David and Alice, it would give him some idea of the problems that lay ahead for the girl.

David stood so he could lean over her, ready to give her a kiss if she was receptive. Jon stood also to get a better look at the situation. Slowly

Alice began to open her eyes. She moved a hand up to cover her eyes because of the brightness of the room. She groaned like a person who had come awake after a long, long sleep.

Ever so gently, David ran his finger down her cheek. "Alice, sweetheart, Alice, I'm here for you."

She moved her had so she could look at who was there. Jon noticed her repaid breathing and one of the machines in the room to which she was attached, showed an elevated pulse rate. There was some distress there, how much, remained to be seen.

"Water, uh water," Alice whispered. David reached for the cup and bent the straw so she could take a sip. She flinched slightly but accepted the straw anyway.

Alice's eyes moved around until she saw Jon Morris. "Mast, uh, Master Morris, what uh," words or strength failed her.

Jon Morris softly put his hand on her shoulder. "I'm here to see you. We were worried about you and I've come to make sure you're okay. David called me and told me some of what happened to you and if there is anything you want or need, just let me know, okay?" Alice nodded and a bit of a smile almost made it to her lips.

"Sweetheart, I'm here, I'm not going anywhere. Okay?" David said, hopefully. She shifter her gaze to David and her pupils dilated. Jon caught the change and took it as a sign she was almost afraid of her fiancé.

The door to the room opened and a nurse and Agent Walker entered the room. "Why was I not told she was awake," the FBI agent said forcefully. "You all need to leave so she can give her statement."

While the nurse checked her vitals, Jon Morris faced off with the agent. "I am this girl's therapist. Up until about two minutes ago she was still not awake. She has solely addressed her desire for some water and to ask why I was here. If you are going to question her, you'll do it in my presence and with her lawyer in attendance."

"Fine, I'll leave the guards on the door and until she talks to me, her visitors will be limited to doctors and hospital staff. Call her lawyer and we can begin the statement." Agent Walker turned on her heel and left the room.

David stepped to the window and made the call to Cecil White. "Yes, Cecil, Walker was in with us, Alice just woke up and the FBI want a statement from her. Can you get her lawyer over her so it's all done on the up and up?" David waited for the reply, "splendid, splendid. I'll wait for you."

They didn't have to wait long. Cecil White came in with a man David had never met before seeing him on the plane the Houndsford Security people had taken to Boston to rescue Alice. Derek Johnson was Alice's attorney and was probably in his late seventies. Chairs were brought in and David was asked by Agent Walker to leave the room, the other people, Cecil White and Jon Morris were told to stand away so the FBI agent could put her recorder on the bed where everything that was said could be taken down and later typed up into an official statement. Cecil White also put a recorder on the bed for the security company's lawyers.

David stood in the hall between the two agents guarding the room. He needed to wait until they were finished to get back to his girl. He saw Evie and Amara exit the elevator and went down the hall to meet them. "The FBI are in with her to take her statement." David told them. "I just don't know what I can do for her right now, she looks so helpless," he ran his hands through his hair and sadly looked to her friend. "Our wedding, it's," at that moment he sat in one of the chairs and put his head in his hands.

Evie and Amara both put a hand on his shoulders trying to comfort him. "Things will work out, you'll see. I've known her most of my life and she's strong, just give her time and the help she needs," said Evie. "Does she know a therapist or someone she can talk to about what happened?"

David looked up, "actually, someone she saw a few months ago is in with her now. I called him and he was happy to come and kind of, you know, give her the help she might need to sort it out in her mind."

Evie and Amara sat with him as they waited for the people in Alice's room to leave. Time ticked by and after almost an hour, the door opened and the lawyer and Cecil White left the room followed by Agent Walker. Jon Morris stayed in the room with Alice. Seeing David, Agent Walker motioned for him to come back to the room she had used earlier as an interview room.

"She's a little shaky on some of the details, but I think we have enough. There is, uh, one thing, however," Walker said, "she said it a couple of times and we found it on the laptop in the office of The Arabesque club, our forensic people found a deleted email she said she sent to a friend. It says, "ask David why he would sell me". That is pretty disturbing and I want your take on this. Why would she think that would be true?"

David paused then said, "Damian tried to convince her that I didn't want her and that she belonged to him is my best guess. I've never done anything nor given her reason to believe that this was something I would ever do. I'm not in the business of selling people, I'm a healer."

The agent tapped something on her tablet, sniffed, and replied, "we're done here then. I may have to do a follow-up with her sometime in the future, but for now, go see her." David thanked the woman and went straight for Alice's room. The FBI guards followed Agent Walker down the hall and into the elevator.

David went into Alice's room and saw Jon talking softly to Alice and her responding in something akin to a quiet whisper. Jon motioned for David to leave the room and he did. Out in the hall, the lawyer and Cecil White cornered him and they went into the interview room to talk.

"We haven't been formally introduced," the lawyer offered his hand to David, "my name is Derek Johnson. I've been the Blake family attorney for many, many years." He chucked, "in fact my father was the one who originally drafted the will for the estate Alice inherited on her twenty-fifth birthday. We've never met but she has had nothing but good things to say about you." David shook the pro-offered hand and sat down.

Cecil White pulled a folder from his briefcase. "Since her abduction, we have done some investigating of our own on this case and everything you have said jives with what we found. But this girl is quite well off and Mr. Johnson here, as her attorney, was wise to have this kind of insurance for her in case she was in this kind of situation. She shouldn't be unprotected now or in the future. When the two of you marry, what kind of protection will you be suppling for her?"

David thought about what he was being told. "I can protect her. Once we are married, she will have me to make sure she is safe."

"Dr. Khoury," the lawyer began, "I've no doubt but what you place Alice's safety as one of your primary duties as her husband. But you are not married as yet and what or who will protect her when she goes shopping or out with friends for lunch? Mr. White here has looked at the new house you've built in the country and found the security there totally lacking. What happens when you're at the hospital for long hours and she's at home?" the lawyer sat back down, "how will you protect her when you're working?"

David opened his mouth to speak but simply bowed his head. He needed to keep her safe and once they were married, she wouldn't be the only one with money that would tempt a kidnapper. There was no way he could make her safe and the words of his Uncle Maurice came back to him. His main job was to protect his family and his family's honor. He had spent the last few years looking after himself and not ventured into the larger concept of family. When they were married, Alice would be his family, well, her and their children. He looked to Cecil.

"When, uh, when Alice and I get married," he started, "well, there is a legacy which I will inherit from my great grandfather. He left a will that entailed his estate to the next male in his direct blood-line. I'm that male heir and it's located in a bank in Switzerland. I don't know how much it is or what all it is, but from what my gran told me, it is probably quite something what with compound interest and all." He looked to the lawyer and then back to Cecil. "I guess what I'm saying is maybe we should look at some security for the house and us."

The lawyer patted his arm, "son, it sounds to me like you need some help. Talk to Mr. White here and he can tell you how to get started. If you want, my grandson is taking over the Blake file when I retire next year. I can have him call if you need help on that type of business. First, though, we need Alice protected and the estate budgets for that so don't worry about the cost."

David got mad, "damn the cost, she means more to me than money, I'll listen to what you say and then we can get to doing what needs to be done." The men talked on for a few minutes, actually Cecil White did most of the talking. By the time Jon Morris stuck his head in to get David, there was the outlines of a plan to protect Alice and David.

David crossed the hall to Alice's room. Jon was again sitting by the bed and she was sitting up with a tray of clear liquids in front of her. When he entered, she put down the broth she was drinking and looked at David. Jon patted her arm, "remember, this is a safe place and you can say anything you want here. Do you want me to stay or leave?"

Alice looked from him to David, in a quiet voice she said, "please stay for a bit. I need to speak to David, but I want you here too."

David went to her and put out his arms to hold her but she backed up and pressed herself into the bed. He simply sat next to her. An awkward silence grew in the room. Jon tried to break the tension. "Alice, is there something you want to say to David?"

Alice turned to look at the man she was promised to, loved, and was preparing to become his consensual slave. Tentatively, she reached out a hand, David sat still and waited for her touch. He looked in her eyes and saw something there he didn't understand. A light brush of her fingertip on his arm and then she withdrew her hand. "David, why?" was all she said.

"Alice," David said. "Can I hold your hand?" She stared at him and then nodded her head. Gently he took her hand and placed it in his. "You asked me why, but I need to know what why you are asking." He felt her begin to withdraw her hand but he continued to hold on to her. "If you want to know why Damian grabbed you for your hotel room, I can tell you that."

For the next several minutes he told her about how he knew Damian in the past and the reasons Damian was giving for thinking David *owed* him something. He told it all and left nothing out. "Does that cover the why or is there something else you need to know about?"

Shakily she asked him, "David, he said you sold me to him and then he sold me to this other man. His name was Jaffar or something. When you stopped the car and talked to him, uh, when he rolled the window back up, he told me that he might have to give me to you, but I belonged to him, he paid for me and he would get me back." By the time she said the last, tears were streaming down her face and her voice wasn't even a whisper. Sobs began to rack her body and David tried to hold her while she cried but she took back her hand and wouldn't let him touch her.

David looked to Jon. "David, she has had a trauma and I don't think, in her mind it is over. Let me spend some more time with her and I'll see what I can do." David smiled at his friend, told Alice he would be here whenever she was ready to see him and left.

Security

The discussion about safety had been very sobering to David. Alice had trusted him to keep her safe. All of the time he was pursuing her he'd told her he wanted to keep her safe and when it came to a real threat, he hadn't fulfilled his promises to her. He needed to think and he went to his father for advice. Jon Morris was with Alice and he'd told David that he'd call him when it was time for him to come back. This gave David the time he needed to see his dad.

Alex and Cora Khoury had been calling every day to see if they could help with Alice, but besides giving them an update on her condition, he'd not spoken to them all that much. Now, David needed his dad's counsel or at least as a sounding board. His mom was cautious with him, not knowing if he would again become the distant son he had been for all of those years before Alice.

Cora Khoury had seen a softening in him since that disastrous night when he'd first brought Alice to the house as his fiancé. She and her husband hadn't handled that at all well and the ramifications had been swift and brutal. It was Alice who had insisted on taking her with them to shop in New York for the wedding dress and also the way she was included in the wedding planning. When she saw her son this first time since getting Alice back, her heart could have broken.

David and Alex retired to her husband's study to discuss something and she busied herself in the kitchen with making coffee and putting some of her son's favorites out so she might tempt him to eat something. Cora could tell her son wasn't taking care of himself with what was going on with his fiancé and now he needed his mom to help get him some sustenance.

In the study, David was relating to his father what Cecil White and the lawyer, Derek Johnson had told him. "Dad, I just don't know about all of this. Geez, I'm a doctor, not a politician or rock star that needs to be followed around by gun-toting security crews. I know my wife, uh, future-wife, comes from money but not really the extent of it. I don't even know what I'm supposed to be inheriting when we marry. Nobody has ever wanted to talk about it. I'm kind of at a loss on exactly what I'm dealing with."

Alex Khoury was distressed over the anguish he saw on his son's face. He was happy he'd finally felt he could come to him with a problem, but wished it hadn't been this kind of a problem. "I can ask around about security people. There's a guy I know that has been in security for several years, he used to know your Uncle Maurice. In fact, Maurice used to do some work for him from time to time."

David had always known there was something that kept his uncle in such good shape. You didn't have the kind of skill-sets he had without using them now and then. He'd always wondered where Maurice's money came from, he guessed security might have been the answer. "Okay, dad, I suppose we can start there." There was, however, the other question. "You know, dad, there is something I want to know. Now I've never asked because, well, I did say something to mom when I was a teenager and she told me never to ask again. It's about great-grandfather's estate. I want …"

Alex held up his hand to stop his son, "and you want to know what it is, right?" David nodded. "Well, we never wanted you to know before you were eligible, you know, married. Your mom and I discussed it when you first asked and we didn't want you to know because we wanted you to be a success in your own right, under your own steam so to speak, without thinking you didn't need to study or work hard because that would always be there for you." He stopped to think about what he would say next. "I don't know everything that is there, all I know is it will be more than a match to what your future wife has now."

David was stunned. This was something he was going to have to think about. It turned out, there were a lot of things to think about. Suddenly, he felt his cellphone vibrate in his pocket. He looked at the message. It was from Jon Morris and was telling him to come back to the hospital. He made his excuses to his father and hugged his mother on the way to his car.

At the hospital he found Alice napping and Jon sitting beside her bed. When the therapist saw him, he came out to the hallway so they could talk without disturbing the girl. "She's resting now," Jon told David, "We talked a lot this morning and I think it tired her out. This incident has triggered some stuff she needs to deal with, feelings that has made her keep people at arm's length where she didn't have to become too attached to them. I know she has the one girlfriend, but other than that, no family and only you." David nodded.

"And, I take it, she wasn't really too keen on you at first either." It was a statement more than a question and Jon continued. "Everybody in her family, well except for someone in New York who is or may be a real aunt, is dead. She feels abandoned. The abduction and Damian Horace trying to convince her you had sold her just played right into the abandonment issues." He looked straight at David, "she feels like you deserted her, sold her, didn't want her, and is almost sure that you will do that in the future when she no longer satisfies you or you find someone you want more than her."

David began to protest but Jon wasn't finished. "David, it's not about you. I know you are crazy in love with this girl, you were going to marry her and collar her as your consensual slave. I get that, this is the kind of commitment men like us don't take lightly. But for her, she has to believe it and understand that you aren't just out for what you can get from her and then going to leave her in a ditch when you get tired of her. This is what you are up against and this is what we have to work on from here."

David ran his hands through his hair in frustration. "So, what do I do? I've told her how I feel, damn I just built a house for her out in the country where she can do anything she wants and we can live our life as Master and slave. I just don't," he looked at his friend, "tell me what to do."

Jon put a friendly hand on his shoulder to comfort him. "David, firstly, she needs to open up to you about the abandonment issues. Let her tell you in her words in her own good time, she also needs space. She can't be inundated by people wanting to know what happened to her or when the wedding is going to be back on."

David understood. He was already getting those calls from family and fortunately his mother was fielding them for him. He just couldn't deal with any of that right now, he needed to get his girl back to his bright, smiling Alice. "So, what do you suggest? Can I take her home and wait for her to come round or what?"

Jon shook his head, "no, no, you can't think about taking her home now. It would be too much pressure on her. She needs to ease into this. I don't want to keep her here. She is well enough to go home but I was thinking, I have several extra rooms in my house and a friend, Dixie Ferris, who is a retired nurse. I can have her come and stay and she can take care of anything Alice might need. I will be there to help her with any mental issues that might crop up." He noticed the rather sour look on David's face. "Of course, anytime you want to come see her will be fine, kind of ease her back into the relationship."

"Is Dixie lifestyle? I wouldn't want Alice to lose all of her training." David said.

Jon laughed, "David that girl is not going to lose any of that. I think it was her training, the things you did with her, that helped her get through that thing with Damian. And yes, Dixie is lifestyle, she was a sub for many years until her Dom started having dementia and she could no longer care for him. He's in a home over near Oak Ridge."

"I don't like it, I mean no disrespect to you, but I just don't like the idea that I can't take her home with me." David looked over at Jon and sighed in resignation. "But, you're right, she shouldn't stay here and I don't want her going someplace else. So, I guess, your place it is. Can I at least go in and sit with her and visit with her or are you taking her now?"

"No, no, no. I want her to stay here for the night. Wagner wants another round of blood tests and the tox screen has yet to be finished. I'll take her tomorrow." He needed to sooth David too, "you go sit with her and when she wakes up. Talk to her and let her know you're always going to be there for her." The two men shook hands and David went in to sit with his girl.

She was so beautiful. David could sit and watch her sleep for hours. The peace and calm it gave him soothed his own mind. It allowed him to think about what needed to be done. However long it took for her to get well, it would be worth it because she was worth it. He had been prepared to accept her as his consensual slave and as her Master he would be responsible for her body, behavior, and attitude. It was his duty to keep her safe, both mentally and physically. He would not shirk his duties or obligation just because things had gotten so *crazy*.

Between the road to the turn off of the new house there was plenty of land to build a small house. The brush had been cut back some when the fence was put up but the main screen of trees and undergrowth still acted as a barrier between the road, the fence, and the clearing where the house was. In his mind he had the outline of what he wanted to do to help keep his bride safe.

Taking out his phone, he sent a text message to the man he had commissioned to design the house. He asked him to give him ideas about building a gatehouse of about thirteen to sixteen hundred square feet that would have three bedrooms and two bathrooms. Within minutes he had an answer. Yes, on the gatehouse. David answered, *make it look right and get it done fast.*

If they had to have security, he would put them there. All of the stuff they could need and the people, the gate house would be their base of operations. When his father would tell him he had some people ready, he would at least have a place to put them.

Alice began to stir and he put the phone away. He took her hand and lightly held it. She opened her eyes and looked at him. She didn't pull away this time and her eyes did not show fear. She looked more like the Alice he had seen the night before all of this had happened. "Hi," David whispered. "I'm happy to see you, my sweetheart."

Alice licked her lips with the tip of her tongue, "hi yourself. Are you alright, Sir?"

David's eyes started to tear up. With all she had been through and she was thinking about him. "My sweet girl, I am fine now that you are back with me. Can I get you anything, water, food, anything?"

"Mm, no, I am a little hungry but I think they only want me to have soft food or something. Water would be nice and," she blushed.

"Tell me, tell me, what do you want," David encouraged her, "whatever it is, let me get it for you."

Whispering, she said, "I hate this gown. I want to sleep naked."

David laughed, "I love you; but you can't sleep naked here, I will bring one of your gowns so you at least don't have this scratchy thing to sleep in." He rubbed the fabric between his fingers. "Yuk! I don't know how anyone could wear this!" his exclamation made Alice smile.

"I've been thinking," David began. "I am going to build a gatehouse between the fence and the screen of trees and undergrowth that makes the property where our home is private from the road. I've been advised by several people that you need to have more security. For both of us actually, and this is where we can put them and still have our own privacy away from people." As he spoke, he watched her closely for any signs of distress at what he was saying. Finding none, he continued, "Jon, Master Morris, is going to have you stay with him for a few days. A friend of his, Dixie, is a nurse and she can look after anything you need. Talk to him Alice, this has been a trauma and you need to get through it mentally, not just physically."

"Master Morris said something about that to me. I don't know," she replied hesitantly, "but, I guess if you say it is for the best then I'll go. Not for too long, though," She shifted in the bed, "what about, uh, you know, the wedding?" she dropped her eyes. "I guess it was a mess. Now what do we do?"

"Alice, my love, we do whatever you want. If you want to run away and get married in Vegas or go down to the courthouse and get married before a judge, we can do what and how you want." David brushed the hair from her face. "First you get better, then we can do all the other things. I'm not pushing you to do anything before you're ready. I love you and want you too much to risk something ever happening to you again."

Alice pulled her hand away and looked David in the eyes. "You can't guarantee that. That man, the one I was sold to, he said I belonged to him, he paid for me and he would get me back. He will come for me and I don't know how you stop him." A tear escaped from her eye and dropped on the cover of her bed. "I, uh, know, you uh, didn't sell me, that this guy Damian was just saying that, but this guy paid money and he is expecting to get what he paid for, me."

He reached out to hug her but she offered her hands for him to hold. "The reason we are getting some people to do our security is because of these kinds of threats. The FBI knows who he is and some other people also. I will not let anyone hurt you like that ever again. If I have to spend every minute of the day with you, which for me would be heaven, I will. They or he or anybody will have to come through me to get to you."

"Just let me worry about the threats and you get better. I need my Alice back to how she was before. I even have a new idea for your collaring, but not until we are married. Church first, dungeon later." His phone vibrated and Alice looked toward the pocket where he was keeping it. "Don't worry, I'm not getting that. From now on I want my time to be for you."

The door to Alice's room opened and a girl came with a tray of food. It was dinnertime and the grimace on Alice's face told him she wasn't quite pleased with what was under the lid on her plate. David, seeing the look on her face pulled out his phone and punched in some numbers. "Yah, mom, Alice is awake and needs something to eat," he listened for a moment, "no mom, soft for this meal. Yes, dad can come too."

David put his phone back in his pocket and turned to Alice, "mom is bringing you something with a bit more flavor than this and dad's coming too. They have been so worried for you. Mom especially. I was over there earlier and she was in tears over what happened to you."

Alice's eyes flew open in surprise and she pulled her hands away from David, "they don't know about the club, that place where they took me and what they did to me, do they?" She put her head in her hands.

David hugged her, "shhh, no baby, they know nothing about that. They know you were taken, abducted, by someone I once knew, but not the details of anything." She finally began to relax in his embrace. He looked down at her head. He wanted to kiss her so badly, but knew it might be too soon. The words of Jon rang in his ears about taking it slow with her and letting her initiate the first contact and how much she felt comfortable with.

Later, when his parents entered the room, they found David sitting on the side of Alice's bed with his arms wrapped around her. They put the food on the tray table and the rustle of the bags brought Alice fully awake. She had dozed off in David's arms.

Cora, David's mother, put some things out for her and Alex motioned for David to join him in the hall. "You two go talk a bit, I'll see that Alice gets some real food to eat," his mom said. Turning to Alice, "this is a lemon soup that is one of David's favorites. And, I've made some baked flan for you to have for dessert." Cora put an arm around Alice's shoulders, "don't worry, we've got you, you're a member of the family sweetie, the daughter I never had. You just let me take good care of you, hm?"

In the hallway, Alex Khoury and David talked quietly. "Look, son, I've talked to about three different people I know about security and they all said the same thing. If you only need somebody to look after you around here, we can get someone to do that, but this was not a local threat. For that you need someone or actually a big outfit that has all of the resources, personnel, and equipment to manage threats wherever they may come from. Maurice would have been the kind for a local assignment, but you and Alice need the big stuff."

"So, dad, any recommendations? I mean, this is all new to me, I'm just a doctor and this is out of my expertise." David said to his dad, "this guy from Houndsford, Cecil White, was good and I like him, but I don't know." He ran his hands through his hair in frustration at not having all of the answers.

"David, Houndsford was one of the companies that my friends mentioned. There was another, but they were more paramilitary. I don't think we're going to war here, but it is up to you." His dad pulled a piece of paper from the inside pocket of his suitcoat. "I have a number if you need it."

David shook his head, "no dad, I've already got them on speed dial." Alex Khoury left his son in the hall and went to join his wife at Alice's bedside. David pulled out his phone to make the call.

Security Always

Amazing what one phone call can initiate! David was sitting at the table with Houndsford's team of people who would take care of whatever security needs David and Alice might have. It was four days since he'd spoken with Cecil White about his company supplying what was needed to keep Alice safe.

Jon had taken Alice to his home and a retired nurse named Dixie was there with them. Evie, Alice's best friend and maid of honor for the wedding, had to return to Florence, Italy to finish her two-year study. Amara, David's designated best man, needed to return to his practice as a cardiologist. Both had spent some time with Alice before leaving.

David expended a lot of time trying to get things ready for when his Alice could come home, either to the old house of Maurice's or the new home he had built for them. Hidden GPS trackers had been installed in all of his vehicles and even Alice's Shelby was now tagged with GPS.

The architect who was drawing up the plans for the gatehouse had a meeting with one of the Houndsford team and incorporated what was needed into the new build. They had also worked with the same people to modify the new house so the security systems needed could be *there* but *not an in-your-face* there.

Jon kept David appraised of Alice's progress at her insistence. After almost two weeks, Jon said it would be a good idea if David would come to dinner. He accepted the invitation immediately. He'd not been away from Alice this long since he had followed her to Florence after her graduation from university and he was aching to see her.

Jon greeted him at the door and then he and Dixie left for a movie. It was just David and Alice in Jon's house. Before leaving, Jon gave David a wink and smile before leaving him to Alice.

She was a bit slimmer than she had been before the wedding. David didn't know it but Alice had availed herself of the gym equipment Jon had installed on the lower level of the house and she was actually more toned than anything else. She was smiling but still a bit apprehensive about this first truly alone time with David.

The dinner went off well and afterwards, they sat before the fire in the small living room and sipped brandy with their coffee. Alice sat next to David on the sofa, but there was still some distance between them. David had to admit, he was nervous about all of this himself. When Alice got up to put the coffee things away and offered David more brandy, she opted to sit in one of the small stuffed chairs in front of the sofa.

David was really worried now, but Alice said she wanted to talk to him. David nodded and hoped he wasn't going to hear the end of their relationship. Then Alice started. "Being here with Jon, Master Morris, and Dixie has been very good for me. It seems there is a lot more than an abduction for me to work through …" For the next forty-five minutes with no interruptions from David, Alice talked about the night of being taken, the things she saw there, and the feeling she'd had about it all. David had wanted to reach out and comfort her, but even though he'd moved forward in his seat, a mere touch away from her, she'd not moved to meet him.

She told him she understood that Damian had lied to her about everything and that Rachel had been so harsh to her because she had wanted David for herself but felt he had rejected her and was taking it out on Alice. But then Alice moved to things that she had felt even before meeting David. The abandonment by her parents dying when they did and the last one, her aunt's heart attack when the last close relative was stripped from her, leaving her an orphan.

Tears flowed and tissue after tissue was used and discarded. Alice had a lot of hurt that needed addressing and she felt David needed to know everything. "When you first started to train me as your sub," Alice said, "you stated that honesty and communication was one of the most important things there could or should ever be between a Dom and sub and then Master and slave. You needed to know all of this. I think, at least as far as I know, there is nothing else about me you don't know." She took her first sip of the brandy by her side and then continued. "Now, if you still think I am worthy to be your wife and you want to collar me as your slave. I think you should take possession of me again. I'm sorry if I may be a bit skittish at first, but it's not you, but what happened to me that is the culprit. You, I have never stopped loving."

Before David could take her in his arms, however, there was one more thing she had to talk about. "David, uh, the labia clips you bought in New York for me, uh, I don't know if," she started to tear up again and he could hear the tremor in her voice. David reached out and this time she put her hands in his. "I, uh, Rachel and Damian made me wear some and he led me by a leash through that club for everyone to look at me," she said in a rush, her body shaking, "I just don't think I can ever wear something like that again, not now and maybe not ever."

David enveloped her in his arms and sat her in his lap. "Oh, my sweet, my heart breaks for what you have been through. Consider the clips gone, I will never use them again." He held her and rocked her like a hurt, lost child. He whispered to her and stroked her hair. They kissed and he brushed kisses on her cheeks and hair. They were reconnecting.

Jon Morris and Dixie came in more than an hour later and found Alice asleep on David's lap. Jon showed David where to put Alice to bed and then the two men sat in the kitchen and talked. "She really opened up to you, huh?" Jon said. "I knew she was getting there, but I didn't know she would go that far. She's doing good and I think now I should see the two of you together, just to get her and you, you know, ready for whatever future you two want to have."

"Look, I know I can't push her and I think I know just what kind of damage she suffered at Damian and Rachal's hands. Even if there hadn't been any earlier trauma of losing everyone in her family, that alone would have fucked her up, bigtime. As it was, geez, it is a lot." David said as he was having a late coffee with Jon.

"Now," Jon said, "you have to be very sure that you are prepared to accept all of this about her and go forward. Don't let what happened to her taint her in your eyes, remember, she was not at fault here. She says nothing happened, no trace of anything untoward happening to her has been found, but you know they, the people who took her, are going to try to make it look like it was something she wanted to have happen. This sleaze that says he bought her, he's still out there also, and who knows what may happen in that direction." Jon was watching how David was taking all of this in. "Make damn sure you are all in on her, never make it her fault for anything, before you take her back into your life. She wants you and is committed to you, but if something happens, something you were both comfortable with before that gives her pause, don't use this to make the blame be on her. Just back up, give it some time, and try again another day."

David was hearing everything Jon was saying and knew he had to be more careful with Alice than he had ever been. But Jon was not finished. "Now, all of that being said, you also can't tiptoe around her or she will think you see her as tainted by all of this. You two are just going to have to find your way through this together. I think if you can come a couple of times for the next couple of weeks, I can give you some couple's sessions that might really help before she leaves with you permanently."

A couple of weeks weighed against the rest of their lives together was a small price to pay if it was going to give him his Alice back and David agreed. He went back to Alice's room and kissed her on the forehead but she didn't stir. Jon was at the front door to wish David goodnight, "you know, I think that is the soundest she's slept since she's been here. This talk with you has really done her a lot of good."

"It's done me a lot of good too," David said as he shook Jon's hand and bid him goodnight.

The two weeks of couple's therapy worked wonders and Alice asked to come home. David spent most of the two weeks wrapping up his work at the hospital and planning what he wanted to do with his professional time. He knew of several doctors who had been through marriage after marriage and divorce after divorce and he didn't what that for his life with Alice. She needed someone who was going to be there for her when needed but not in a hovering, smothering way, but just *there*.

Before Amara left to return with Evie to Florence, David had talked to him about coming in with him in a private practice. Alice had told him that although Evie loved being in Italy with Amara and his parents, she was really missing being home. David knew Amara was going to ask Evie to be his wife and a ready-made position in the United States would give him a good reason to bring Evie back as his new bride with a job waiting for him. Amara was excited by the idea and told David he would get back to him.

The main idea behind working in private practice with Amara was that the hours would be much better for them both. With a good office manager who was proficient in medical practice management, they could do the doctoring and the business side of it would be handled by a professional. There was a nice sized standalone building close to the new house but in town that would be a good medical-office conversion. It had ample parking and no steps which would be good for patients who had mobility issues. It was even on the bus line. They could have privileges to work at two local hospitals.

David had put his condo up for sale and a new doctor in the OB/GYN department was interested in buying it because it was so close to the hospital. He finally decided that a temporary move into Uncle Maurice's house would work well while he finished out his leave notice at the hospital and he and Alice could make plans to get married and move to the new house.

At the last session with Jon and Alice, he told her of his plans and she was pleased he was going ahead with them. They had talked about him doing something like this when he had taken her to see the new house for the first time. She was happy to think he would be on a more regular work schedule with a private practice and the idea that Amara might be his partner and Evie would be home, was just the extra wonderful news she liked about the whole thing.

The day after the final session David picked up Alice and took her home to Maurice's house. A friend from the local lifestyle group told David about a service sub who liked to clean houses. He interviewed Lisa a few days before bringing Alice home and she seemed to be okay with coming in once a week to clean the house. He had her in to clean and tidy the place the day before to make sure the house was ready for

Alice's first day home. Lisa had done a great job and if Alice wanted to keep the arrangement, he was all for it.

On the way to the house, David told Alice about Lisa and she was fine with it. It would give her more time to catch up with the work on her trust she'd let slide when she was at Jon's and there was still a wedding to plan. The wedding, though, was something they still had to discuss.

Leaving the safety of Master Moriss's home was making Alice a little anxious. She loved David, loved him deeply and yes, she wanted to marry him and as far as being his consensual slave, she wanted that as well. The sessions with Jon Morris had helped her understand the deep need she felt to serve him and their relationship. Her happiness was tied to David and their dynamic or at least what their dynamic would be as Master/slave.

Coming home after so long away was emotional for Alice. There was a point in the abduction and her sale to Jaffar when she thought she would never see this house or the dungeon ever again. As David brought her things in from the car, she slipped into the closet to remove her clothing, put on the heavy collar and cuffs, and find her Zen spot where she could take off her *outside self* for her *inside self*. As she stood before the full-length mirror on the back of the closet door, she saw herself, naked for David to take her anytime or way he wanted and the thought made her wet. The tragedy in The Arabesque and Damian had been delt with and David was her future. She closed the door and turned to see her Sir.

When David walked into the bedroom, he saw his Alice emerge from the closet. He dropped the bags on the floor and took her hand. Holding her at arm's length he looked at her and his heart was full of love for his girl. His girl, home at last. He pulled her to him and crushed her against his chest. The toned muscles of his chest and his strong arms enveloped her and he raised her chin so he could kiss her. When their lips met the surge of want and the need they both felt crackled between them and the kiss was long and probing.

David lifted Alice onto the bed and stood above her while he shucked his clothes off and they were thrown to the floor. He straddled her. His hands massaged her breasts while his mouth again claimed another kiss. His fingers rolled and pulled her nipples into hard points. He got off the bed and pulled a silk scarf from a drawer. He tied Alices hands together and affixed them to the headboard of the bed. She giggled as he did so.

"What my girl, did I tickle you when I bound you to my bed?" David whispered.

Alice nodded, "not at all, I've been dreaming about you doing this to me for a long time. I have craved you doing just this to me."

"So, you've dreamed about me doing this," he said just before he sucked a nipple into his mouth and his teeth grazed her nipple as the areola pebbled. "What about this?" he said as he pulled her legs wide and his fingers found her seam and parted it to play with her clit. "Maybe, you wanted me to do this in your dream." He slipped two fingers into her pussy and curved them up to find her g-spot. She moaned against his chest. He had her just on the edge of an orgasm when he pulled out and said, "no my love, I don't want you to come yet, that will happen when I am inside of you. Did your dream include that?" He loosened the silk scarf that bound her to the bed and flipped her over, he pulled her to the edge of the bed and told her to get on all fours.

He put his cock into her and held it still, letting her become used to his size. With one hand he found her clit and began lightly tapping on it but she was so close to the edge he just held her by the hips and he began to move in and out, slowly at first but his need was also great and he began taking her a bit more roughly. "Please David, don't hold back, I want it, fuck me David, just fuck me as hard as you can," Alice was almost screaming his name as she begged him. "Let me come, please, fuck me and let me come."

This was all David needed to push him into a frenzy. He had wrapped her hair around one hand and with the other began thumping her clit again. The first orgasm she had blasted from her and her muscles tightened around his cock. He kept the steady beat against her clit and the orgasm continued to surge through her. He was almost at his climax when he took his hand from her clit and spanked her, first on one side and then the other, over and over until her ass cheeks were a bright, cherry-red. He went back to her clit as she climaxed again. He joined her as he pushed deeper and deeper into her and pumped load after load of cum into her. His cock continued to pound her as the cum filled her and started to ooze out around him. His thumb pulled one more orgasm from Alice as the last of David's load pulsed into her.

David pulled out and grabbed a handful of tissues to put under Alice where his cum was sliding out of her. He pulled his phone from his jeans and made a video of his seed dripping out of her pussy and the swollen clit to which he'd given such loving attention. The last thing was her cherry-red ass with his hand prints and the video was complete.

Alice began to get up but David told her to stay. He untied the silk scarf from her hands and then told her to stand. "Don't shower until tonight, I want to see my cum glistening on your thighs for the rest of the day. And tonight, I will use you in the dungeon, I think you and I have both missed our play." He pulled her to him and kissed her again, "put your stuff away and take whatever time you need to get caught up with any of your other things. If I stay in here with you, like this, we'll be in bed all day and I know you have some work you want to get done. We can take this up after playtime."

Alice was happy to be back in her life. The more she did around the house, the time she spent catching up on the estate business, the further away the horror of her non-wedding day was. She knew, however, a new wedding date had to be planned and she began to question just how much wedding she really wanted. Everything that she and Cora had worked so hard to make just perfect had been shattered when she was abducted by Damian and sold to Jaffar.

She asked David about the things from the hotel suite where she had stayed before the wedding. In particular Alice wanted to know about the dress. He hadn't told her how he had found it on the floor with shoe marks that could only have come from the only female in the room, Rachel, when she was taken. David had sent it to Kami Worth but the rips from the heels of Rachel's boots had torn into the delicate silk and could not be repaired.

When they talked about it, Alice was almost relieved about the dress. As much as she loved it, she would be reminded of what had happened every time she would see it and wedding pictures with her in that dress was not something she wanted to look at in the years to come. A few days after her return to the old house, she and David sat in the glow of the fireplace in the kitchen drinking coffee after a delicious evening meal. Alice brought up the question of the wedding and David was happy she had been the one to start the conversation.

"I know we had a beautiful wedding planned and everything was going to be exactly perfect until it wasn't. I don't think I could go through the planning of something like that again. If there weren't so many people who would be disappointed if we didn't have a big wedding, I'd say just take your parents and go to Florence and get married there with Evie and Amara as our witnesses." Alice said, "what I can say is we do a smaller church wedding. For the reception, I'll see what hotel ballroom might be available and have it there. The wedding planner is still wanting to do the event and I think with your mom's help we can do this, but now we need to talk dates."

David beamed, he was so happy she wanted to finalize wedding plans which would help fix, well, at least partially repair, what had been broken by Damian. "I suppose it depends on when we can get a place to have the reception. It's up to you love, this is your big day. As you know, my big day will come after, when I formally put my collar on you." He did have one thing he needed to know. "Are you sure about all of this, the wedding and the collaring? If you have any qualms, we should address them before we try this again."

Alice was surprised, she thought David would have been happy about her wanting to move forward with their lives. "I'm sure. I can get Kami to do a dress, the wedding planner will be paid for the majority of the rest of it, and I'm hoping your mom will help. I'm ready."

"I'm not worried about the wedding part, I know that can be done with no problems," he said, "what I am thinking about is the collaring the next evening and the, uh, the robe you will wear and the part where you will be naked. Are you ready for that? I don't want to do something that will trigger you and start giving you nightmares about Damian or The Arabesque."

She placed her hand on his and looked into his eyes. "My love, I'm ready to be your wife and look forward to you accepting me as your consensual slave-girl." She lowered her eyes and whispered, "you already have my heart and I want everyone to know that I, officially, belong to you."

Weddings and Such

The next few weeks seamed to fly by and Alice and David returned to their busy schedules. The gatehouse was coming along nicely and Houndsford Security was interviewing and assigning people to work with David and Alice on security details. At first it was strange for both of them to have people around them every time they left the house to go somewhere but it soon became routine and the people were nice, professional, and unobtrusive.

A venue was found and the church was the only problem. The church was booked on the days when the venue was open and vice versa. The solution was for David and Alice to have their small church wedding a week before the actual reception. As it happened, it worked out better than having everything on the same day.

Evie returned to the States after her time in Italy working on her PhD came to an end. She'd accepted Amara's proposal and her parents planned on a wedding in the beginning of the coming year. When David and Alice had their wedding, Amara would again come to be David's best man and Evie was there to be maid of honor. David and Alice were asked to be the same for Evie and Amara.

The small wedding in the church was a beautiful affair. The dress Alice had Kami make for her was a white silk charmeuse that clung to her figure and had a deep drape in the back with a draped neck in the front. A short court train kept the fabric pulled backwards as she walked down the aisle. David wore a new bespoke tuxedo of black trousers with a black silk cummerbund and a while dinner jacket and black tie. Evie was in a lovely dove grey silk charmeuse with a plunging neckline and Amara was resplendent in dress trousers with a white dinner jacket.

David's father closed one of his restaurants for the evening and the dinner was attended by about thirty people. That night, David and Alice spent their first night in the new house. The fireplace in the living room, a big sectional especially made for the space, and a bottle of champagne was all the couple needed to christen the fact they were man and wife. The new security system had been set and they were safe in their new place. The reception would be in a week and the official collaring the day after.

Their wedding night started late and with no work for either of them for the next few days, David took full advantage of not having any interruptions. When he carried his bride over the threshold, he went straight to the living room and put her over the back of the sofa. Alice was giggling as he raised the back of her dress. "Good to see my wife is without her underwear," he said as he spanked her on her ass. "Now I'm going to fuck you like never before." He growled as he rubbed her ass, then began spanking her in earnest. Whack after whack rained down on her until her butt was red and David's handprint was clear to see. He spread her legs and slid a finger in her to see if she was ready for him.

Alice was dripping and David's finger in her was almost enough to make her come. When she heard his zipper, she knew she was about to get her prize. He thrust his long, hard cock into her and filled her. Roughly he pounded into her, deeper and deeper, while his fingers circled and thrummed on her clit. She begged him to let her come but each time she got close, he pulled his hand away and instead played with her breasts. Soon, she felt him coming close to his own release and he again circled her clit until they both found their release together.

When David pulled out of her, he watched as his cum dripped out of her and puddled on the terrazzo floor. "Up wife, go take off the dress but leave the cum. I want to see it on you and I'll be putting lots more in you when you get back from the bedroom." Smiling at her husband, Alice removed her shoes and ran to the new master bedroom to change.

Alice had already chosen the place in one of the closets where she would change and put on her cuffs and heavy collar she would wear around the house. Naked except for the leather she wore, cum glistening on her thighs, she went back to the living room and David. The hungry look in his eye sent a jolt of desire for him straight to her core.

David had removed his dress clothes and put on a short robe. As he was sitting on the sofa, the robe was gaping open and his fully erect cock was plain to see. Alice dropped to her knees in front of him. Taking his penis in her hands she slid her fists, hand over hand, up and down his length. She kissed the head, licked the precum from the slit, and took him in her mouth. Up and down on his cock, licking, swirling her tongue, and sucking his head. Slowly at first, but then going faster. She took him as far down her throat as she could while one hand cradled his balls, gently massaging them, and scratching his scrotum.

He put his hands in her hair and moaned as she increased her speed then backed off to a slower movement. Soon he was fucking her mouth because he had to come and the pace she was making was driving him crazy with his want to release. He finally pulled out of her mouth and positioned her in his lap as he plunged his cock into her. Now it was for him to set the pace and he proceeded to raise her up and plunge her down on his cock. She begged to come and he told her to wait, he was almost there with her. They again came together when she orgasmed and the muscles in her silken passage squeezed his cock as he drove deeper into her and he exploded. She leaned into him and put her head on his chest. Both were spent, at least until the next time.

Sometime that night the champagne was opened, a couple of half empty glasses and the almost full bottle were all that was left in the living room to show they may have drunk another toast to the wedding. Mostly the carnal activity was in the bedroom and dungeon. Neither one could have said how many times David had taken her or the times Alice tempted him to make love to her or just fuck her with all he had. By the early hours of Monday morning the two finally collapsed into bed sated and happy, at least until they wanted to go again.

Mid-morning on the Monday after the wedding, a black limousine was stopped at the gate. The man who was the passenger was asking to talk to David Khoury. One of Houndsford's men, Marty Johnson, left the temporary trailer that sat behind the unfinished gate house and went to question the occupants of the car and then called to the house to ask David for permission for the man to enter. David told the security guard to bring the man to the house in one of the golf carts they used for their patrols.

David stood at the front door and waited for the man to approach. From what he could see of the gentleman, he was in his late fifties, expensively dress, and held an overstuffed briefcase and a laptop bag. David extended his hand, "David Khoury,"

"Klaus Marche of Stellear and Moss, Washington. DC." He said as he reciprocated by extending a well-manicured hand. "Can we go inside please?"

"Absolutely," David stepped aside and led the man into the nearby study. "Come this way and I'll have coffee sent into us." He looked toward the kitchen and asked Alice if she could bring them some coffee.

Nothing was said between the two men until after Alice brought in the coffee service and closed the door behind her.

Mr. Marche pulled a card from his wallet and let David see his driver's license to verify that he was, indeed, who he'd said he was and the card to show the name of the law firm he represented. David kept the card and returned the license.

David began, "so, Mr. Marche, what can I help you with?"

"First, Mr. Khoury, I need to ask you a few questions as a way of identifying you. I represent a private financial institution in Switzerland. Certain accounts have been holding a legacy which may be yours, if we can get the matter of your lineage sorted. Do you, perchance have a copy of a will that names, and I quote, "the first direct male heir of the line of Michael Khoury, graduate of the Sorbonne, born in Tripoli, Lebanon, citizen of Saudi Arabia", end quote?"

David chuckled, "I do, and I have a diploma, and several other papers which have passed from generation to generation. They were just gifted to me on this Saturday last when I married my wife, Alice. I'll get them for you." David left the room and a woman stepped in and stood by the door.

"Good morning, Miller," he said to the guard as he left the room. "I won't be a minute."

"Sir," said Janet Miller, Houndsford operative, and designated officer on the domestic detail. Her eyes never left the stranger in the house.

In less than two minutes David returned with the documents. He opened an old wooden box with a small key and revealed the papers he had listed. Some of them were very obviously old and the wax seals on the diploma were cracked and the ribbons frayed, but everything was still legible. The documents that were in any language but English had a recent translation appended to it. In the bottom of the box were also recent photocopies of both the documents themselves and the translations. He handed them to Mr. Marche.

"If I may," Marche said. He took his cell phone and photographed the originals, slipped the SD card out of the slot on his phone and plugged it into his laptop. He brought the pictures up on the screen and compared them to copies that had been furnished by the bank. He waited. Within about ten minutes a green screen replaced the one he had been looking at so intently. "It seems the clients are satisfied that your documents are legitimate."

Marche reached into his briefcase and pulled a large file from it. He placed it on the desk in from of him and looked at David. "This is your copy of the account from Hochuel and Fraiche of Geneva, Switzerland, they are the legal firm who represents the banking house where these accounts have been held." He turned the file around and slid it across the desk to David. "If you will open the file to page one, we can start."

David looked up at Miller and nodded to her. She stepped out and took up a post sitting by the door to keep anyone but Alice from going in. For the next three hours muffled sounds, mostly the voice of Marche, could be heard droning on through the door.

At one point in the presentation, David picked up the phone and asked for more coffee. Miller knocked once and came in pushing a tea cart. David asked her if the driver had been given anything, "yes, sir, he is in the guard-trailer with Johnson having his lunch. Can I have anything brought in here for you?"

David looked at Marche who simply shook his head, "no, I guess not, thank you." Without a word but a nod to David, Miller left.

Finally, David had reached the last page. It was a letter, written in his great grandfather's hand. David read from the translation.

To my Heir,

I have lived a good life, worked hard, created beauty in the sand, and loved my wife and child. If you are reading this, then you must be the one for whom this legacy is intended. My wife came to me with a dowery, my daughter married with one, and my little grand-daughter will have one when she is married, the women have all been provided for. But you are the man, the one to whom this is given and it comes with obligations.

You will look after and guard your family, be judicious in everything you do, create beauty, love your church and God, do not fail. It was commanded of us to be fruitful and multiply but multiply only to the extent of your means my son.

Since this will has a clause that you be married in order to inherit, I pray you have taken a good woman to wife and you be blessed with sons and daughters. Remember they are your true wealth, love them, teach them, and raise them up to be a credit to our name. Do not let them be spoiled by what they have but grateful to be able to help others.

Live well my boy.
Michel Ragab Khoury

David closed the file. He was stunned by what was in it. Looking at Marche he said, "now what? What am I supposed to do?"

Marche smiled for the first time since leaving the car he'd arrived in. "Dr. Khoury, I have only been the messenger, but I think you might wish to get a local attorney, one you trust, who can advise you on this," he tapped the file. He pulled a thumb drive from the side of his laptop and placed it on the file. "This is the computer copy of what is in that, I would give it to my lawyer, accountant, whoever you will get to manage your estate." He put his laptop back in its bag, stood, and took his, now much lighter, briefcase. "My work is done. I'll bid you good day."

David called to have the limo brought to the house then walked Marche to the door and watched him get into the car and drive away. Alice came up behind him. He pulled her to him and put a protective arm around her shoulders. She put her hand on his back and could feel some tension there.

Arm in arm they went back to the study. David told her about the estate of his great grandfather, the extent of it was even now, just settling into his brain. "He had liquidated everything he had, houses, land, farms, the lot, into cash and gold. It has been setting there since early 1964 just earning interest. The original deposit in cash began as thirty-seven million dollars and I don't know how much in gold, and at an average eight percent compound interest, at least according to the documents, well, it's over four billion. The bank has asked that we don't move the gold or if we want to, turn the gold into currency then move it out. However, I don't know, it's been there all these years and from what it started as to what it is now, believe me, compound interest really works!" David squeezed his wife's hand, "there is also a considerable amount of jewelry in a safety deposit box that is earmarked, *For your wife*. That, I think we'll have sent here."

Alice watched as he put the documents back into the box. "You know, with what your great-grandfather has left you and the approximately three billion that my family's estate is worth, I guess we won't have to worry about how we will put our children through college," she said, "maybe your wish to put a baby in me every year isn't so farfetched after all. And besides, you standing there looking all sexy like that, I think we should at least practice on making them, if that is alright with you."

David had been standing by the desk looking at his bride. Trying to look nonchalant, he had his hands in his pockets as he watched in awe as his wife put the words to his dream of a big family. Finally, he took the box that held the documents, put the thumb drive in it, and Alice took the file. The safe was in the bedroom and David led the way as they went there to put the things away. He would have to think about the contents later, what Alice had said about her estate, and her comments about a baby every year, but right now there was a wife to bed and her idea of practicing making babies was something he wanted to pursue.

Collaring

The ballroom was turned into a fairyland. The chandeliers, which hung from the ceiling, were decked out with trailing vines, satin ribbons, and white flowers, each table had a centerpiece of gardenias and baby's-breath and were tied off with royal blue ribbons. There was a dance floor but currently a string quartet played softly in the background. David, Alice, Amara, and Evie had not yet appeared but the rest of the guests sat speaking in a low murmur. When the two couples appeared at the double doorway, Evie and Amara entered then when David and Alice walked in, the music changed to *here comes the bride.*

The guests stood and the two couples made their way to the front table where David's parents were siting along with the Orthodox priest who married them the week before. Applause came from the assemblage, mostly family of David's, but some collogues and a few friends. This was the party they had expected at the first attempt and they would all make the most of it. At each place setting sat a delicate porcelain cherub with Alice and David's name and the date of their wedding, a favor for the attendee to remember the occasion.

The meal was good, better than many had for their receptions, but the best the hotel could do with such short notice. Toasts were given and a couple of speeches, one by David's father about how proud he was of his son and welcoming his new daughter. Amara's speech was just as sincere, but did contain a funny story about David that made everyone laugh. When Amara finished, he directed everyone to look at a screen which came down from the ceiling.

Anyone over a certain age and even some younger people who had seen her show in re-runs could recognize the woman who appeared on the screen, Lucy Rose. Her tribute and blessing to her great-niece was funny, tearful, and straight from the heart. She might be old and pretty frail, but her presence on the screen was still something to marvel at and everyone applauded her little speech.

The screen receded back into the ceiling and the band changed while the cake was being cut. Alice fed David, and David fed his bride. A server cut the cake and everyone was given some. David and Alice took their places for the first dance, then Amara and Evie began the dance. It would go on until late into the night, but the newlyweds still had to receive the personal well-wishes of the guests.

Two large, comfortable chairs were placed next to the head table and David and Alice took their places. A line formed of cousins, aunts and uncles, friends, and collogues. Each wanted to shake hands, some slipped David or Alice an envelope which was put into a box on a table that sat between them. By the time the line had ended, Alice and David both shook out their hands to ease the ache caused by shaking over three hundred hands.

All gifts, those sent to the house, to David's new office, or sent via his parents, had been discreetly scanned to check for any possible threats. A table had been set up in the ballroom, near the door, where late gifts could be placed. Two of the security staff assigned to the event, picked up the table and moved it to a room down the hall. It was their job to examine each and vouch for the safety of it before it was touched by David or Alice.

One package, wrapped in silver paper and tied with a white bow, gave one of the female agents pause. A portable scanner had been set up to examine and photograph the contents of each gift, the agent saw the outline of metal chains and circles of varying sizes. She wore gloves while handling each item and carefully removed the card from the gift and opened it. She turned off the scanner, took the photo from the printer, and with the card in hand, and went to the supervisor.

Cecil White had come to take charge of the security for the festivities and reassess the situation of Houndsford's agents and their role in the security of the Khoury couple. When the agent in charge of the parcels came to him with the photo of the gift and the card, he told her to secure the items while he had a word with his client. "Take the package, card, and envelope out to the trailer and tell them I want fingerprints ASAP."

Cecil made his way into the ballroom and waited to catch David's eye. While David was making his way to where Cecil was standing, the package in question was being opened carefully by a technician in the command trailer at the side of the hotel. Finger prints and any other possible traces that might identify who might have handled or touched the package or contents, even breathed on the card, was gathered. Before the gift could be shown to the happy couple, it would have to be cleared as being safe. What the meaning of it was, was far from clear.

When David reached Cecil, they left to stand outside in the hall where it was not quite as noisy and easier for David to hear what Cecil needed to tell him. "David, we were scanning the gifts that were brought here for the reception and one of them is something you need to see right now." He led him outside to the trailer and he sent one of the women agents to tell Alice that David would be right back.

The interior of the trailer was mostly dark to make it easier for the man who watched the various camera feeds from around the outside and inside of the hallway and ballroom. Cecil told him to pullup the camera that had been trained on the gifts table and locate the frames that showed the person who had put that particular gift on the table. Further back in the trailer, a table with a lightbar above it held the package, the paper it was wrapped in, and the contents.

Seeing it, David knew exactly what the contents were and who had sent it. He was furious but before he could say anything to Cecil, the man charged with the watching the video feeds said, "Boss, look at this." David and Cecil moved to look over the man's shoulder. They expected to see video of who put the package on the table but it was of David's father, Alex Khoury, walking toward the trailer and knocking on the door.

Alex Khoury was worried. It wasn't like David to leave his bride and seeing a security guard standing next to her bothered him. It was time for him to find out what the problem was. The guard at the door directed him where to go and now, standing in the command trailer for Houndsford Security, he was sure something bad was going on.

Alex started to pick up the card but was given a photocopy of it instead. Oh, yes, fingerprints. He read the note:

> *I bought her, I own her, she is mine. These are the only things my slave will wear when I come for her and I will come. She is my property!*
>
> *Amin F Jaffar*

Alex looked at his son and then to Cecil. The man watching the video called Cecil back while David and his father had a quiet but heated word.

On the video feed, a man was shown, frame by frame, placing the package on the gifts table. He was youngish, probably no more than twenty, and not in very good shape. He was dressed in the uniform of a delivery company. Cecil was on the phone with the office of the firm in minutes. The man who gave them the package was in a hotel room not far from them. Cecil called someone and told them to go to the hotel and question the man in the room. The description the delivery man gave didn't match Jaffar, but any link to the man would be useful.

When the men arrived at the hotel, the person of interest was not in that room and according to the hotel records, the room had been unoccupied for the last two days. Other avenues were being pursued.

Alex Khoury had seen enough. He left the trailer and took out his phone to make a call. Fifteen minutes later he put the phone back in his pocket and smiled. David was his son, Alice was his wife, and the children she would produce would be his grandchildren. A man takes care of his family.

David's collaring ceremony for Alice was not taking place at the dungeon in the new house but in the one at Master Moriss's home. With the kind of security the Houndsford group was providing, the outside of the property at the new house would need to be cleared for security purposes. For many members of the group who would be in attendance, it would not be fair to them or for their privacy. Being in a BDSM group was no longer against the law in the state where they lived, and it wasn't considered a mental disorder any longer, but the people that would be at the collaring were from several professions which would frown upon its members taking part. To guard against that, there were strict protocols which were in place to safeguard identities.

David arrived at Jon's place early in the day to work with some of the other Masters and Doms to prepare the dungeon space for the ceremony. In the old house that Maurice had given him and where Alice had lived while he was training her, Alice was being bathed, pampered, and prepared by some of the slaves and subs of the group so she would be ready when it was time to take her to Master Moriss's house. All of the women were going dressed in fine gowns which they would change out of when the time came.

Houndsford did supply the twenty-seat luxury transport van that moved Alice and the other women from Maurice's to Jon Moriss's house. Houndsford would supply the security outside of the building, but not inside. The van driver let the ladies out at the front of the house and then left. All had been delivered as ordered.

Inside, a catered dinner was served to all of the guests. Master Moriss's roll as host fit him well and everyone looked to be having a wonderful time. When the meal was finished and the caterers had left the kitchen like they'd found it and driven away in their truck, the men went into the dungeon.

The Masters and Doms were in their dress-leathers or if they weren't part of a leather house, in tuxedos. David was resplendent in his bespoke suit and his number two called his sub to tell her they were ready for the ceremony to begin. The lights in the dungeon were lowered except for one pin light that shown down from the ceiling in the middle of the room.

The place where the light illuminated was normally where a large St. Andrew's Cross would be placed, but earlier in the day some of the men had moved it out of the way and in its place had put a raised dais with a plush cushion and a small table. Above the dais was a tract secured into the ceiling that held various chains and one of the chains had been placed over the platform to be used later in this solemn occasion.

At the doorway of the dungeon, lined up in two rows, the subs and slaves of the Masters and Doms waited to come into the room. Dressed in matching robes of diaphanous fabric, slit up the side, open in the front, and tied with a sash, the ladies entered, each carrying an electric candle which gave off a muted glow. In they filed to stand before their respective men and as one, they sank to their knees into a formal kneel on the cushions in front of them. Alice and her attendant then entered and Alice took up her place in front of David on the cushion provided.

David's second stepped forward and handed him a sheaf of papers. The Contract. The Master/slave contract that David and Alice had discussed for the last several months after she had formally asked that he take her as his slave. A totally non-binding and unenforceable document in every state of the United States, it nonetheless was an oath of honor, trust, and loyalty that was more important to the parties to it than any marriage license a state had yet to produce. The man and woman who would sign this document entered into a relationship that would far outstrip any marriage agreement ever pledged.

David's second started reading. After each paragraph he asked each of them if they agreed.

> **Preamble:** *The essence, spirit, and intent of this contract are based on the simple notion of a structured personal relationship between the parties identified hereinafter … the Master … exercise responsible control for the day to day living of both parties … the slave being fully informed of the responsibilities and expectations placed upon her, consensual without coercion or undue influence agrees to obey the Master in all asked of her …*

> **Master's Responsibility:** *… accepts the responsibility of slave's body; to do with as he sees fit … undertakes responsibility to define slave's behavior and attitudes and teach, then enforce these elements to please him … to care for the well-being of slave … arrange for her physical and emotional safety … accepts responsibility to fulfill slave's needs … responsibility to treat slave properly; to train,*

punish, and use slave for pleasure and useful service …recognizes slave's desire for this relationship structure and works to build a life of peace and tranquility together, through intimacy, affection, honest communication, trust, love, and romance, embodied in structure …

Slave's Responsibility: *SLAVE agrees to submit completely to Master in all ways … are no boundaries of place, time, or situation in which slave may willfully refuse to obey the directive of Master without risking corrective measurements and punishment by Master, except in the activities relating to boundaries … agrees that once into this Contract, her body belongs to the Master, to be used as seen fit, within the guidelines defined herein … agrees to be useful, utilizing her skills, talent, knowledge, and experience in service, taking direction and using initiative within the structure of rituals, protocols, and rules taught by Master … agrees to please the Master to the best of her ability, with her primary focus now Master's pleasure, needs, and wants … Slave will be loyal to her integrity and Master …*

Agreements between Master and slave

WE agree that our relationship will always come first in our lives. We will not put work or other outside interests before our relationship …

Page after page and sub-paragraph after sub-paragraph, he finally came to an end. "Master David, do you, of your own free will, agree to all that has been read to you?" David said he did and the second turned to Alice, "rise Alice, do you, of your own free will, agree to all that has been read to you?" In a whisper she also said yes. "Step forward and prepare to sign."

The attendant who had come in with Alice came forward with a small bowl, feathered quill pen, a small knife, and some bandages. She put them on the table and then stood aside. The second took the knife, nicked a finger of David's and one of Alice's and let the drops of blood fall into the bowl. The attendant wiped the fingers clean with alcohol and put a bandage on them. David's second mixed the blood in the bowl with some ink and water.

David took the pen and scratched his name on the contract. He put the pen back on the table. Alice came forward, picked up the pen, and put her name on the contract also. She went back to kneel on her cushion. The second took the table away and brought David a soft bag.

David stood before Alice and told her to bare her neck. From the bag he took a beautiful collar which he had specially made for Alice. It was a white-gold circle that, when locked, made it look like there was no beginning or end. He placed it on Alice's neck. "This is my collar; you will wear this collar for as long as you are my slave. I am the only one who can remove it from you and that will only happen if you need medical care or you are released. With this collar, I signify that I accept you as my consensual slave. Rise and hug your Master."

Gracefully slave alice stood and for the first time said, "yes, Master." David took the opportunity to kiss his slave-girl. He placed a white-gold ring on her right hand which was engraved with the date of the collaring and contract signing. But now, the ceremony needed to be completed.

David looked at his slave-girl and turning to the people in the room, "in times past when a Master took a new slave, the first thing he did to impress upon them the fact he was their owner was to whip or cane them." Several people around the room nodded in agreement. The attendant took the robe off of Alice leaving her totally naked. Looking at his girl he said, "alice, bend and brace." Hearing the command, alice immediately bent at the waist and steadied herself with her hands on her knees. She knew what was coming and hoped she would not disappoint her Master.

David took the carbon-fiber cane from the second. He took several practice swings with it and the 'whoosh', was distinctive sound it made. "Who are you alice, spell it for me."

With the first strike on her ass, alice began, "S," one strike with the cane, "L", two and again, "A", three again and etc., "V", four, "E", five, "A", six, "L", seven, "I", eight, "C", nine, "E", ten." His girl never cried out or wavered. David was so proud of her and he told her that when he bent down to whisper in her ear and to stand.

David stood before those assembled and alice, "It is common that at this time in the collaring, a slave is branded with a cold brand. As you all know, this kind of brand is not permanent so we have a renewal ceremony about every five years to reapply the brand." David nodded to his second who stepped forward and lowered the chain.

Alice had heavy leather cuffs on her wrists and ankles. The second took the wrist cuffs and attached them to the chain above their heads and then attached the ankle cuffs to bolts in the floor. He raised the chain so she stood on tiptoes but her legs were spread wide. David then stood up and said to the group, "For Alice, I want something that will last for our lifetime together."

David's second brought forward a brand with David's initials on it which had been heating in the fireplace. David put the hot brand on his slave's inner thigh, marking her for life. She screamed in pain because of the area was so sensitive, but then pushed into the pain. The attendant sprayed deadening liquid and antibiotic on alice then the second placed a bandage on the burn.

David took his girl down and held her in his arms. The assemblage erupted in applause and cheers. The heavy leather cuffs were replaced by two white-gold anklets and similar ones on her wrists. She would wear these when going out while the new leather cuffs and a new leather collar would be worn, along with the gold one on her neck, in the house.

Alice rested in David's lap for another hour before he dressed her for the ride home. Out on the street, David and Alice got into the backseat of a town car and left for the new house. In their room, he removed her clothes and bandages, lifted her into a tub of warm water, and got in behind her. Lovingly he bathed her, dried her, and put her to bed.

David put a leather cuff on her right ankle which he locked into place. He put a clean bandage on the brand. He affixed the rope that bound her to their bed, pulled her to him, and they slept in each other's arms.

In the still dark hours of the morning, David felt his love rouse from sleep. In the moonlight streaming through the windows he saw the twinkle in her eyes and it fired his need for her. His hands caressed her body, played with her nipples bringing a gasp of pleasure from her. "I don't want to hurt you love, are you sure?" he asked.

Alice nodded then found her voice when she moaned a 'yes' in answer.

Being particularly careful of the bandage, David's hands continued their journey over Alice's body. His mouth claimed hers' as his tongue took control of her and the need they both felt deepened the kiss. One hand continued to play with her nipples, pulling them, rolling them between his fingers, and pinching them just hard enough to make Alice's moans of pleasure more pronounced.

David's other hand went to her core, parting her lips to feel the wetness. Delving a finger into her pussy he put one finger to fuck her and the thumb to circle her clit and tease her close to orgasm. She had always been so responsive and this morning was no different. Reluctantly he broke from the kiss and moved down Alice's body. Licking her nipples, kissing her bellybutton, and onward to her pubic area.

Finally, he removed his hand from her pussy and his mouth took over. His tongue darted in and out of her passage then flicked her clit. He made it a pattern, flick, dart, lick, flick, and etc. Alice was close and he eased back just enough to keep her on the edge but not enough to push her over into an orgasm.

He pulled her to the end of the bed and turned her over. "I want you to come with me my love," he said as he pushed his cock into her silken passage. He waited for her to adjust to him and then he began pushing in and pulling out. He held her by a handful of hair with one hand and the other was on her hip. He was careful of the bandage and continued his movements, speeding up and then slowing down. When he couldn't wait any longer, he told Alice to play with her clit as he pounded into her. He felt her coming as her muscles tightened around his cock and pushed him into his release.

David filled her with his seed as he continued to stroke into her. He replaced her hand on her clit and pushed another orgasm from her and the tightening was enough to milk the last of his cum from him. He carefully laid her down with his cock still in her. As he started to become flaccid, he reluctantly slid out of her and went into the bathroom to bring a damp towel to clean her.

Alice looked into his eyes and smiled. "I love you my Master and thank you for making me yours." He held her in his arms and they resumed their night together.

David and Alice, Master and slave, joined in peace at last.

Epilogue

min Jaffar didn't stay long in anyone place. In years past, when he was active in arms-trading, he'd lived aboard a 747 which served as his home and office. Now however, he had houses and apartments in several different countries and various cities plus his private island off the coast of Panama'. The penthouse in New York was discrete, very comfortable, and owned by one of his shell companies. The people who traveled with him consisted of bodyguards, a cook, an assistant who handled his papers and communications, and one or more girls who warmed his bed.

In the afternoons, while he sat on the balcony and enjoyed the park below, he liked to sip tea and indulge in a piece or two of his favorite dessert, baklava. Normally the cook kept a ready supply of the sweets that were made by a special bakery in Lebanon, but cook was running low and before the next shipment could arrive, he bought a pound of them from the only baker in New York who could produce anything close to the ones from Beirut. Cook had given strict orders that no pecans were to be used since his boss was deathly allergic to that particular nut.

Jaffar left one of the girls, Lilly, sleeping. Post lunch sex with the girl was becoming boring and it made him think about the one he'd bought from Damian. It had been a week since he'd sent his own, special, reminder to her that she was still his property, even if she had married that nobody doctor. He dressed and told his head of security he wanted to see him in his study.

"I want plans made to go get my property. Work it out and give me your best ideas by tonight. Oh, and tell cook I want my tea on the balcony as soon as possible." Jaffar ordered the man.

Cook prepared the tea tray with his boss's favorite tea, two pieces of the baklava from the New York bakery, and rolled the cart to the balcony. After giving him the tea, he put the sweets on the table where his employer could reach them. Unbeknownst to the bodyguards, the cook then slipped out of the penthouse and left to spend a much needed-retirement in Paris.

Half an hour later, Amin Jaffar was in an ambulance being rushed to the hospital due to an allergic reaction. Agents from the FBI were quickly at his bedside with handcuffs, a warrant for his arrest, and the contents of a bulging file folder with enough evidence of gun running, human trafficking, and large drug shipments, to put him in prison in several countries for life. The penthouse was raided and authorities in numerous countries started confiscating, impounding, and seizing houses, cars, airplanes, apartments, and bank accounts belonging to Jaffar or any of a myriad of shell companies he owned. In the end, he wouldn't have the money to pay a lawyer.

Alex Khoury was sitting in his home enjoying the warmth of the fire in the hearth, his wife sitting beside him on the sofa, and the sound of his stereo system playing some light classical music was soothing. His cellphone vibrated in his pocket and he looked at the message on the screen. He smiled and put the phone back in his pocket. He would call that friend of a friend tomorrow and thank him for the news. He chuckled, feeling like a weight had been lifted from him. His family was finally safe from Jaffar and the thought of future grandchildren warmed his heart. His line would continue.